Four Weddings to Fall in Love

Weddings with the Moks, Book 1

Jackie Lau

First edition: July 2023

Print ISBN: 978-1-989610-31-2

Editor: Ali Williams

Cover Design: Sarah Kil Creative Studio

The Four Weddings

Tessa Dubois & Malcolm McDermitt

Mirabel Mok & Dylan Lowry

Isobel Mok & Daisy Wang

Yvonne Siu & Carl Mok

Chapter 1

Max

"FUCKING *HELL*."

I hear the woman before I see her—I'm busy adjusting the suit bag in my hand—and nearly trip over her leg. She's fallen on the stone path that leads to the hotel on the lake.

"Are you okay?" I ask.

Before I can extend my hand, she jumps up. Her purple dress ends just below her knees.

"Yeah, I'm fine. These shoes just aren't made for running." The petite East Asian lady gestures to her silver stilettos with her bouquet. One of Tessa's bridesmaids, I assume. "Even for walking, they're a fucking nightmare." She pauses. "Sorry."

She doesn't need to apologize for her language, but perhaps she senses that I'm not the sort of person who swears vehemently, well, ever. A quiet "shit" is as far as I go and—

Wow. She smiles at me, and I'm struck by how beautiful she is.

There's a giggle from behind the pink rose bushes. Her gaze snaps in that direction.

"For fuck's sake," she mutters. "The flower girl escaped again, and I'm tasked with bringing her back." She dashes off toward the roses.

I shake my head and continue along the path. Someone else in a purple dress flies out the door of the hotel. Is she also in pursuit of the flower girl, or is there another wedding-related emergency?

God, weddings are such chaos, and I have four to attend in the next three months.

I head into the lobby, check in, and proceed to my room on the second floor, where I hang up my suit and open my suitcase. Still over an hour until the ceremony starts, so I'm in no rush. It's not as if it'll take me more than fifteen minutes to get ready.

My phone rings. It's my parents, so I answer.

"Did you get there safely?" Mom asks.

"Yes," I say, "but traffic was bad so it took almost three hours."

I would have called within the next few minutes if she didn't call me first. I never want her to worry, and I do my best to ensure she doesn't have to worry about *me*.

"Max!" My dad's voice bellows over the phone. He's the louder of my parents by far. "How's it going? Any pretty brides-maids?"

"The wedding hasn't started yet," I say crisply, even though I'm thinking about the woman I saw earlier.

"I think that means yes."

"It does not."

We chat for a few more minutes, then I tell him that I have to get going. Before I get dressed, I glance out the window, toward the small lake. Chairs are set out for the ceremony, and the wind whips around some gauzy material at the altar...and the flower girl is running down the aisle, pursued by two bridesmaids, two other women, and a Canada goose.

My lips twitch.

Weddings aren't my cup of tea. Not because I don't believe in love—I do—but because there are so many people, and I get asked about my own romantic prospects. It's gotten worse recently, thanks to the fact that I'm thirty-five and single, I suppose.

Plus, something usually goes wrong. The groomsmen have horrible hangovers and look like death warmed over during the ceremony; the maid of honor slips and falls onto the cake; the father of the groom gets punched in the face by his brother, due to some quarrel that started twenty-seven years ago; the photographer is trying to hide a dead body. Obviously, the latter hasn't occurred at any weddings that I've attended...at least I don't think so. But anything can happen at a wedding.

Even if it mostly goes according to plan, the parents of the happy couple might freak out over something minor. Maybe the peonies in the bouquets aren't quite big enough, or the canapés aren't the perfect temperature.

The next three weddings I have to attend are those of my cousins. All of Auntie Gladys's kids are getting married this year, and she's definitely the sort who'd make a big deal out of small imperfections. My mother and Auntie Gladys don't get along at the best of times, and she's really been trying Mom's patience lately, constantly calling my parents about one thing or another. So while I'm happy for my cousins in theory, I'm not looking forward to those weddings.

But this wedding, my friend Malcolm's, doesn't involve family. It should try my sanity a little less, though the long drive wasn't a good start to the day.

I head outside twenty-five minutes before the ceremony is due to start.

"Max Mok!" Bryce slaps me on the arm with too much force. "I thought it was you."

Bryce has always delighted in saying my full name. He's one of Malcolm's friends from university, like me, but the two of us aren't friends, not even on Facebook—I deleted his request—and I haven't seen him in years.

"Hello, Bryce." I hope if I don't say anything more, he'll leave me alone, even though I'm fairly sure that hope is in vain.

"You here alone?" he asks.

"Yes."

He introduces me to his girlfriend just as a string quartet starts playing an Elton John song. "Don't worry, we'll find someone for you tonight."

The last thing I need is Bryce's help, but rather than expressing my thoughts on the matter, I simply thin my lips.

"Tessa has a friend who's also a structural engineer," he says.

"Mm-hmm." I suppose he imagines us bonding over concrete, rebar, or similar.

I take a seat. Bryce, unfortunately, sits beside me, his date on his other side.

I'm pleased when the ceremony starts right on time. The groom and the groomsmen enter first, followed by the bridesmaids. The first bridesmaid bears a strong resemblance to Tessa, and I assume it's her sister.

The second bridesmaid is *her*. The woman I met in front of the hotel.

Unlike earlier, she's not swearing and glaring at her shoes; no, she's walking regally down the aisle, pink and white bouquet held in both hands, a smile on her face. I'm next to the aisle, and when she walks by, I swear the air changes a little, though that might just be the breeze off the lake.

Her skin is pebbled with goose bumps; indeed, it's not a very warm day for early June, and while the bridesmaid's dress isn't what I'd call skimpy, it has significantly less fabric than my suit.

The sunlight brings out the brown highlights in her dark hair, which is in an updo. Her expression is determined, focused. I rather wish she'd glance my way, but she's looking straight ahead, chin up.

"Max," Bryce hisses, and I cringe when a few people turn in our direction before looking back at the bride.

Right. I get to my feet. I'm supposed to be standing because Tessa has made her entrance with her father and mother.

I was just too focused on the bridesmaid.

I wish I knew her name. I could ask Bryce later—he tends to know everyone—but the thought of having to ask him anything makes me shudder, so I nix that possibility. Besides, it's not like I'm going to approach her. God, no. Say a cheesy line, ask if she wants to dance, stammer when she mentions a husband or wife? Nah, not my thing.

Yes, I'm a little shy. I might not show my anxiety on the outside, but I feel it nonetheless, and I'm not at my best when I'm surrounded by a hundred or so people, most of them strangers.

I turn my attention toward Malcolm and Tessa, who are staring adoringly into each other's eyes. They met on a dating app seven years ago and got engaged five years later.

For a brief moment, I consider talking to the pretty bridesmaid at the reception. I do want what Malcolm and Tessa have, even if it's something I rarely admit out loud.

"Ahhhhh!"

My thoughts are interrupted as the flower girl lets out an ear-piercing scream for no discernible reason and races back up the aisle.

See what I mean? Weddings are full of chaos.

Chapter 2

Kim

It was a hectic day preparing for the wedding, especially since the flower girl was a bit of an escape artist, but aside from her scream, the ceremony went well. I didn't even mind the personalized vows.

If I ever get married—I won't, but let's pretend for a moment—I will not be writing my own vows. They're usually cringeworthy, though these were better than average and mercifully short.

And now, my friend is married, the bridal party pictures are complete, and Tessa and Malcolm are taking couple's photos in the picturesque garden by the lake. I wrap myself in a shawl and grab a fruity cocktail from a passing server.

"Thank you," I murmur before going to huddle by one of the heaters. It's fucking freezing today, and the ceremony and cocktails are outdoors; dinner is under a big white tent. I thought early June was supposed to be warmer than this.

Still, I'm happy to be here for Tessa, I truly am, even if marriage isn't something I want for myself. As the newlyweds approach the patio, Malcolm's mother intercepts them, reminding me, once again, of why the thought of marriage makes me want to break out in hives.

When you marry someone, you also marry their family.

I already have one family to deal with; I don't need another. I can't imagine liking someone enough that I'd willingly put up with that for years. My perfect man has no parents or siblings or other relatives.

Okay, that doesn't sound right. I wouldn't wish that someone lost their parents at a young age. But I suppose I can wish that he appeared on the planet as a fully formed adult.

See? My perfect man doesn't exist.

Long-term relationships involve a lot of giving, without receiving much in return. For example, giving your time and energy to another family and dealing with a mother-in-law. I broke up with Troy five years ago, and I'm still recovering from my dealings with his mom, who clearly didn't think I was good enough for her precious son.

Yep, I don't need that nonsense.

Some people look for love at a wedding, but not me, though I *am* interested in some fun between the sheets if an opportunity presents itself. I'd very much like to end my dry spell.

Once again, my eyes find *him*.

He's easy to spot, in part because there aren't a ton of other Asian people here. (Tessa's mother is Asian and her father is white; she grew up in this mostly white small town.) But even if it weren't for that, he'd stand out. He's tall, and he has harsh, beautiful features.

I think *striking* is the right word.

He also has glasses, which look particularly sexy on him.

Unfortunately, the first time we encountered each other, it was right after I'd fallen on the ground, and he heard me swearing up a storm. Still, I noticed he was attractive, and now that he's wearing a well-fitting gray suit, he's even hotter, which I hadn't thought was possible.

Tessa told me that he's Malcolm's friend from university. His name is Max, he's single, and he's also a structural engineer. She waggled her eyebrows after she said that, as though us having the same profession was a good sign.

But I don't want to talk about concrete tonight. I just want to get laid.

My body tingles with excitement.

I try to catch his eye, but he's not looking in my direction, and for some reason, I have the sense that he's purposely not looking, yet is aware of exactly where I am. From the way his eyes bored into mine earlier, I think he likes what he sees.

Thankfully, this purple dress isn't godawful. I doubt I'll be able to wear it again—it definitely looks like a bridesmaid's dress—but it could be worse. It could be that pink monstrosity I had to wear for my cousin's wedding more than three years ago, the last wedding I went to before the pandemic.

Trust me, it was impossible to flirt while wearing that. At least with this, I have something to work with.

Hungry, I grab a slider off a tray just as Iris Chin approaches me. She works with me and Tessa. Tessa and I have been there since we finished university, but Iris joined the company two years ago.

"You talk to him yet?" she asks.

"Who?" I say innocently.

She rolls her eyes. "The guy you keep looking at."

"Nah, but I will, don't worry. The night's still young."

I have three more weddings in the near future, but this wedding is a better opportunity for hooking up than the others, for one simple reason: my parents aren't here. The other three weddings involve family friends. My parents have known Gladys and Gilbert for decades, and their oldest daughter is the same age as me.

"You're not going to chicken out, are you?" Iris asks.

"I promise you, I'm no chicken."

There's a cold gust of wind, and I huddle closer to the heater.

"This is the only reason I'm talking to you right now," Iris jokes. "Because you're standing in the warmest place on the patio."

"It really is cold, isn't it?" I say. "How was your drive up today?"

"The 401 was even worse than usual, which is saying something."

Since I'm in the bridal party, I drove in last night, and I managed to time it such that the traffic was only moderately terrible. This is the farthest I'm traveling for a wedding this year, thankfully.

I grew up in the Toronto area, as did Iris. To be honest, I'm glad I didn't grow up in a place like this. The city is more my style—and I suspect this town doesn't have any good dim sum.

"He's looking at you again," Iris says. "Maybe you'll hit it off, and next year, I'll be going to your wedding."

"Oh, please."

"Don't worry, I won't tell Tessa to throw the bouquet straight to you."

I give her a look. "You better not."

The reception proceeds as planned, more or less. The food is good but ultimately forgettable—I requested steak, and we're all served a salad before our main course. Speeches are made. The emcee attempts a few terrible jokes.

I'm not sure anyone planned on Tessa's mom speaking for a full twenty-five minutes, but it's a moving speech. It also has a few moments that make everyone laugh. Tessa embraces her mom afterward, and I think they both shed a few tears—they're closer than me and my mother.

That's another reason I don't want to get married: I hate to imagine what my mother would be like with a wedding on the horizon. Just the thought of her making a speech sends shivers down my spine.

I'm seated at the head table, and Max is at a table with a few of Malcolm's friends from university, as well as a few of Tessa's friends. He's next to a white guy whom he clearly finds annoying. At one point, he glances in my direction, and when I smile at him, he quickly turns away. I doubt this guy will make the first move, but that's fine. I'm happy to make the moves.

Once dinner is finished and the bride and groom have their first dance as a married couple, I saunter his way. He's standing by the edge of the tent, beside the guy who was sitting with him earlier.

"Hey!" I say. "You're Malcolm's friends, right? I'm Kim."

"I'm Bryce." Bryce gestures to the man next to him. "This is Max."

"You're here alone, Max, aren't you?" I hold out my hand. "Wanna dance?"

Bryce walks away, thankfully, leaving us alone.

Rather than answering my question, Max says, "How's your leg?" He has a low, pleasing voice.

"Scraped my knee, but that's covered by the dress. I'm just glad I didn't rip the fabric." I step closer. "I saw you looking at me earlier."

"Did you?" There's not much inflection in his voice, nor much change to his expression, but I sense that he's slightly alarmed by my observation.

"Yep!" I say cheerfully. "Don't worry, I liked it. You look like the star in the drama I'm watching."

Once again, he looks slightly alarmed.

"Except you have short hair," I say, "and you're not, like, the biggest villain in the universe and thirty thousand years old." I pause. "At least, I don't think you are."

Hmm. Maybe I shouldn't have made that silly comparison.

But then he smiles. *There we go.*

"So, you wanna dance?" I ask. "You don't have to move much. Just hold my hand, put your other hand on my waist, and let me do the moving, if that's acceptable to you."

If he rejects my advances, I'll walk away. It's fine. I'm sure I can find someone else—one of Malcolm's cousins was flirting with me earlier, for example.

But as it turns out, that isn't necessary.

He takes my hand and leads me onto the dance floor, beneath the twinkling fairy lights, and excitement sizzles through my veins. He's much taller than me; even though I'm wearing heels, I only go up to his chin. His other hand moves to my waist, and I can feel the warmth of his big hand through the thin material of my dress.

Mmm. That's nice.

I haven't felt anything quite like this in a long time, and the fact that I'm enjoying such a simple touch seems like a good sign for the rest of the night.

When he steps back, my chest deflates. I assume he's changed his mind about this dancing business, but then he removes his suit jacket and holds it in my direction.

"Take it," he says. "You've been standing by the heater and shivering all night."

"So you *have* been watching me." Pleased, I drape the jacket over my shoulders. It's loose—his shoulders are much broader than mine—but I instantly feel warmer.

"Perhaps."

Max isn't the greatest conversationalist, but that's okay. Talking isn't what I have in mind for the evening, and there's something particularly thrilling about getting a guy like this unbuttoned. I have fond memories of a starchy actuary I met post-Troy. Even if I hadn't already sworn off long-term relationships, we never would have worked out. First of all, he literally counted in his sleep, and second of all, he makes Max seem talkative. I felt like I was performing a monologue.

But he knew how to use his mouth in other ways, if you know what I mean, and we had a very good weekend together. I have similar hopes for tonight.

The song ends, and a new one starts.

"I hate this song," Max mutters.

"Yeah? I don't think I know it. Sing the chorus for me."

As expected, the suggestion of singing earns me a glare, but he pulls me a little closer. My heart rate kicks up a notch.

"You'll hear it in approximately nine seconds," he says.

I still don't recognize the song, but that doesn't mean I can't dance to it. I shimmy my shoulders and sway my hips. I hope it makes him think about how I could move horizontally. Or against a door. I'm okay with that, too, but I've recently decided I'm too old for shower sex.

Max isn't moving as much as I am, but he shuffles his feet and keeps a hold on me. Out of the corner of my eye, I see Iris talking to Tessa's father, and she shoots me a thumbs-up.

I return my attention to Max. For the first time today, I feel pleasantly warm. His body heat, his jacket... My hand drifts to his hair, and I tilt my head up.

"Not here," he says shortly, then drags me off the dance floor.

"Where are we going?" I struggle to keep up with him in my stilettos. I can't wait to get out of these shoes.

"I don't know. Away. I don't kiss in public."

Just the thought of his mouth on mine...it's enough to make my skin prickle.

The lake isn't far, but it's far enough that no one can see us clearly from the tent. I figure that'll suffice. When I stop walking, he puts both hands on my waist.

"Lower," I murmur, moving his hands so he's grabbing my ass.

Then I leaned forward and kiss him.

His lips immediately part for me. He tastes of berry vanilla wedding cake. With all the fondant, I found the cake too sweet, but when combined with his mouth...

Mmm.

Under the moonlit sky, strains of music and laughter reaching us from the reception, this could be a romantic moment, if romance were on my mind, but it isn't.

No, I want something different.

His tongue touches mine. He makes an irresistible groan that I want to hear again and again...just for tonight.

He hitches up the bottom of my dress and slides one hand up my leg, squeezing my ass gently. I pull him closer, molding myself against him. My body hums in approval when I feel his erection. This is what I need. Him inside me. That perfectly pressed dress shirt wrinkled on the floor. Hands, lips, teeth, tongue...everywhere. My body spiraling up and up toward its release.

I itch to loosen the knot of his tie, to make him a little disheveled, but I sense he wouldn't like that unless he was behind closed doors, so I leave it. For now.

Yes, I think this is going to be a very good night.

Someone clears their throat, and Max immediately backs away from me. Disappointed, I glance behind us.

"Iris!" I say. *Why are you disrupting me? Can't you tell I was busy?*

Incredibly, I manage not to swear.

"I'm really sorry," she says. "Tessa is tossing the bouquet in a few minutes, and she insisted I find you."

"For fuck's sake." And there it is. "I don't even want to catch the bouquet."

"I know. I told her that, but like I said, she insisted."

"Fine," I huff. "I'll be there in a minute."

Iris nods and starts walking away. But she looks back a few seconds later, and although it's hard to tell in the darkness, I think she shoots me a wink.

I turn to Max. "We'll continue this later?"

Chapter 3

Max

Fire and ice. That's how I think of us.

I'm cool. Reserved.

She's bold. A flame that consumes whatever's in its path.

This is the first time I've kissed a woman not long after meeting her. I haven't made out with a huge number of women. Some, sure—I've had a few relationships—but not many.

Kim knows what she wants, and, improbably, she wants *me*. I'm entranced.

"Why don't you want to catch the bouquet?" I ask as we make our way back to the tent.

"It's a stupid tradition," she says. "Many brides don't bother with it these days, but for some reason, Tessa still wants to do it."

I wonder how often the person who grabs the bouquet actually gets married next. Probably very rarely, but I bet anytime it happens, everyone makes a big deal of it.

"Besides," she continues, "it's not like I want to get married—or even have a long-term relationship again."

"No?" My tone is mild, but I can't help feeling a little deflated.

Not that I was thinking of marriage; I just met her. But I'd considered asking if she wanted to see me again, back in Toronto—does she live in Toronto? I don't even know.

Except now, I suspect she's just looking for a one-night stand.

My heart thumps faster at the thought of that purple fabric pooling on the floor of the hotel room. I've never had a one-night stand before.

And I don't know her. I tell myself that I don't know enough to want more.

Maybe a one-night stand is just perfect for us.

Though as I look at her face in the shadows, her updo slightly askew, I can't help thinking it won't be enough.

I try to banish the thought.

"And you?" she asks. "Do you want to get married one day?"

"Yes, one day." I did get close to proposing a few years ago, but instead, I broke up with my girlfriend after realizing she didn't love me; I just ticked a bunch of boxes, and she was ready to settle down.

I want to be more than a checklist of acceptable traits.

We're nearly back at the tent when Kim says, "What time is it?"

I check my watch. "Just before ten."

"Want to meet me in my room at ten thirty? I'm in three-eleven."

I hold her gaze. "I'll be there."

Bryce waggles his eyebrows when he sees me, and I respond with a glare, although I can feel myself blush. I go to stand on the other side of the space that has been cleared on the dance floor for the bouquet toss. Kim joins the crowd of unmarried ladies. She stands near the back, behind a taller woman who has her hands in the air and looks much more enthusiastic.

"Everyone ready?" Tessa turns around, her back facing the women, and holds the large bouquet above her head. She tips it forward, then backward. Release. The equations for projectile motion pop into my mind—I can't help it.

The bouquet is heading in Kim's general direction, but she steps to the right, away from its path. The enthusiastic woman makes a grab for it. The flowers hit her shoulder and she doesn't quite manage the catch...and now the bouquet is hurtling toward a stunned Kim, who winces as she holds up her hands to protect her face.

Yes, even though she tried to avoid it, she ends up catching the bouquet.

Iris bends over and laughs.

Tessa laughs, too, as she walks over to Kim. "I can't wait to attend your wedding."

"Uh..."

Kim was all confidence earlier, but she looks flustered now.

Did an ex treat her poorly? Is that why a lasting relationship scares her?

My hands clench. For a split second, I'm determined to show her that it doesn't have to be that way. Just a reflex, I suppose. I quickly remind myself that I hardly know her.

But I'm probably going to see her naked tonight.

Fuck.

I need to get out of here before I embarrass myself.

I sit down at one of the tables, watching as people return to dancing. When Malcolm finishes a conversation with a relative—his great-aunt, if I remember correctly—I go up to him.

"Congratulations again." I spoke to him in the receiving line, but that lasted all of three seconds.

He slaps me jovially on the back. "Good to see you, Max." Malcolm is usually in good spirits, but he's particularly happy today—as he should be. "Glad you could make it. We should hang out in Toronto, once I get back from the honeymoon."

"Where are you going?" I ask.

"Paris, then a couple of other places in France. Tessa has always wanted to go."

We talk for another minute. Then I make my excuses, saying something about being tired and needing to turn in for the night. I hope I'm coherent.

Kim is speaking to the other bridesmaids. She's still wearing my jacket over her dress. It makes me feel like I have some kind of claim on her, and I admit, I rather like it.

I return to my room for a few minutes to calm myself down, and once it's 10:28, I head to her room, on the floor above mine.

I'm doing this. I'm actually doing this.

My brother Jon—who's a bit of a playboy and always trying to get me to be more like him—would be proud. Not that I'll ever tell him about tonight, of course.

Just as I'm about to knock, something occurs to me.

Condoms.

I didn't bring any in my suitcase because I certainly wasn't expecting sex to happen, and I curse myself for not being prepared.

I knock, and when Kim opens the door, I say, more brusquely than intended, "Do you have condoms?"

She grabs my tie and pulls me inside.

"Don't worry, I've got you covered," she says, closing the door. She slips off her shoes and lets out a moan that goes straight to my cock. "Those were killing me."

Without her heels, Kim is nearly a foot shorter than me. She stands on her toes, presses a kiss to my lips, and before I can pull her close, she turns around and sashays farther into the room, tugging her dress over her head as she goes.

Oh, fuck.

She drops the dress on the floor, and now she's clad in a strapless bra—light brown, just a touch darker than her skin—and lacy black panties. My cock jerks against my zipper. Her ass is a work of art, and I can't wait to get my hands and mouth on her.

Oh fuck, indeed. How did I get so lucky?

But even as I'm consumed by lust, my brain registers that my suit jacket is hanging over a chair, rather than getting wrinkled on the floor. Good.

"Like what you see?" she asks, in a tone that suggests she knows I do, very much.

"Yes. You're treating my jacket with the respect it deserves." I nod toward the chair.

She laughs. "So you *do* have a sense of humor."

"Of course." I pretend to be a little peeved by her comment, but it's difficult when I can't drag my eyes away from her ass.

I force myself to look away, then remember there's no need to do that. There's nobody here but us, and she clearly wants to be admired. As she should. Her underwear shows an enticing amount of skin through the generous holes in the lace.

"Aren't you going to touch me?" she purrs.

I go over to her, and before I can reach for her bra clasp, she grabs my tie and loosens it.

"That's better," she says.

I try my hand at removing her bra, but like a teenage boy who's never done this before, I'm struggling. I spin her around so I can get a better look at what I'm doing. It's an ordinary clasp, so why am I fumbling? Shouldn't this be simple?

Kim takes pity on me and smoothly strips off the bra, then turns around so I can see her tits. I'm stunned speechless by how gorgeous she is. Small breasts, tight brown buds. I want to squeeze them and suck her nipples, but I shouldn't. My ex hated that.

I straighten up and remove my tie. Even loosened, it was still too constricting. I toss it over the chair and start working on my shirt buttons. Given that it's not very warm today, the amount I'm sweating is rather embarrassing.

I throw caution to the wind and actually drop my shirt on the floor—I know, I know, I'm not sure what's come over me—then set aside my glasses.

"Mmm." She pushes me down so I'm sitting on the bed and runs her hand over my chest. "Very nice."

She climbs onto my lap, and my head is spinning. I palm her ass as she kisses me, her mouth hot and welcoming and eager. When she starts grinding, I squeeze my eyes shut, willing myself not to blow my load prematurely. If only I'd had the forethought to jerk off in the shower earlier, maybe I wouldn't be quite so on edge.

I pick Kim up, set her on her back, and brace myself above her. I run my finger over the edge of her underwear. She nods eagerly, and I slide my hand inside and almost die.

I'm not generally prone to this level of hyperbole and theatrics, but she really does feel incredible. She twists her hips, as if seeking more pressure, and I'm suddenly filled with the urge to flip her over and smack her bare ass, see what kind of noises she makes then.

No, I don't think that would be appropriate.

Instead, I slide down her underwear, revealing neatly trimmed hair. I'm mesmerized by the sight of my finger moving in and out of her body. I thrust more quickly and add a second finger. Gorgeous.

I don't think I can wait any longer. I'm desperate to be inside her, to feel her inner muscles squeezing me. I'm not sure I'll survive it, but I can think of nothing else.

"Where are...condoms?" I stammer.

Chapter 4

Kim

I GESTURE TO THE box on the bedside table.

I'm a touch disappointed that Max asked about the condoms just now. Not because I don't want him to use protection—of course I want to be safe—but for a moment there, I thought he was going to pin my hands against the headboard, and I would have liked that.

This encounter isn't going quite the way I envisioned.

He became clumsy when he tried to unclasp my bra, but it was endearing, to be honest. Like he was so turned on, he'd lost full control of his fingers. Then he slid one of those fingers inside me and just thrusted in and out like a jackhammer, no finesse.

I wish...

Well, I like it rather rough and filthy. A bit of spanking, being trapped against a wall. Nothing extreme, but I like feeling a little used. I enjoy it when a man pushes my head onto his cock...and then goes down on me with relish later; I might enjoy being on my knees, but I don't want it to be all about his pleasure.

If he doesn't want that, though, it's okay—I've had good sex that wasn't rough. Maybe it'll be better once he's inside me, but we just feel out of sync, somehow.

He dips his head and touches his tongue to my clit.

Oh, God. Yes.

But he only gives me a few licks before getting up to remove his pants and boxer briefs. He does look quite nice, his erection bobbing between his legs.

It takes him a while to get the condom out of the packet, though he manages better than he did with my bra. Finally, he sheathes himself and positions himself above me. He pushes inside, just a little.

"Good?" he asks.

I nod.

He closes his eyes as he fully seats himself within me, and then he starts moving slowly. It's enjoyable enough but not incredible. I want to *feel*, but I'm in my head more than I usually am during sex.

As he kisses me, he slips his hand between my thighs. It takes him a few seconds to find my clit, but then he's stroking me, and I think I might be able to come—I usually come pretty easily.

Unfortunately, he withdraws his hand. An odd sound escapes his lips as he shudders.

He pulls out and heads to the washroom, and I try not to feel too disappointed.

When Max tugged me off the dance floor and we kissed by the lake, things were going well. I thought we had a connection; I assumed I was in for a great night.

Alas, it wasn't to be.

He returns to bed and pulls me into his arms. I hope that now he'll finally pay attention to my breasts or try to get me off.

But he just mumbles, "You're amazing," and falls asleep.

Dammit.

I sigh, and then my disappointment morphs into something sharper.

I can't believe this is how my nine-month dry spell ended. Nine months might not be too long for some people, but it's a hell of a long time for me. Last summer, I slept with a bunch of different men, and it was all good fun. Since then...well, I've had a few opportunities in the past several months, but none of them felt quite right. I was waiting for something better.

Not *that*.

I'm pissed.

Seriously, how was I so wrong about him? It reminds me of my lackluster encounters early in university, and I wasn't looking for a repeat of those.

I read an article recently about how few women orgasm the first time they have sex with a new male partner. I don't remember the exact percentage, but it's a bad sign that I'm able to think of statistics at all right now. I do recall that the number was much lower than my own personal experience in the past decade...yet here I am. I wish I'd flirted with Malcolm's cousin instead.

This was not how tonight was supposed to go.

Yes, I know orgasms aren't the be-all-and-end-all of sex, but for me, they're usually part of a pleasurable sexual experience, and I feel like Max didn't focus enough on me tonight. It was too fast, and it just felt off.

I glare at the back of his head, tempted to wake him up and kick him out of my room. Instead, I shut my eyes and try to sleep.

But with the frustration coursing through my veins, I fear this will take a while.

I wonder when I'll finally end my dry spell of *good* sex.

Chapter 5

Max

When I wake up, the lights are out. It takes me a moment to remember where I am, but once I do, my mind is clearer than it was earlier.

I check the alarm clock. The digits glow in the dark room. 12:04.

Shit. I came to Kim's room, completely lost my mind when she took off her dress, and embarrassed myself when I tried to remove her bra.

And she didn't even come.

When I got back to bed, I should have offered to go down on her. I barely had my mouth on her earlier, and I want more. But now she's asleep and...

Shit.

Kim chose *me* tonight, and I felt honored. I bet she knows good sex, and I'm positive I didn't live up to expectations. There wasn't enough foreplay. I should have asked what she wanted and made sure she enjoyed herself more. I shouldn't have immediately fallen asleep.

Dammit. Maybe I'm just not built for one-night stands. Maybe it's just too hard for me to be with a woman I barely know.

I'm usually good at pleasing my partner—I swear I am—but this whole experience was too overwhelming for my poor brain.

I've never slept with a woman on the day I met her. I wasn't prepared. I was focused on not coming too early, but that wouldn't have been the end of the world, if she still had fun.

I wish I had a chance to prove that I really can be good in bed. I'm no sex god, but my girlfriends have been satisfied in the past. I made sure of it.

I doubt she'd want to give me another chance, though. Even if she did, I think I would be too embarrassed to look her in the eyes. How the fuck did I screw this up? She was so amazing...

Too amazing for me, I suppose.

I can't stay the night. I can't imagine she'd want me to stay the night.

Silently, I get dressed—somehow, I manage to find all my clothes in the dark—and vow to head home early tomorrow so there's no chance of running into her at breakfast.

Before I leave, I glance toward the lump in the bed. Kim is lying on her side, facing away from the door. I can't see much with the lights out, but I'm sure her face and naked body will be seared in my brain for a long, long time to come. I'll try not to obsess about my failure, although knowing me, that's a lost cause.

As quietly as possible, I head to the door and step into the hallway. Thank God nobody's around. I'm never going to tell *anyone* about what happened tonight. Since I doubt I'll ever see Kim again, that shouldn't be a problem.

But I hate that I disappointed her, and at 2 a.m., predictably, I'm still wide awake, annoyed with myself as I ruminate about what happened.

I also find myself fearing—as I often do when I'm awake at this hour—that fulfilling a checklist, like I did for my ex, is all I can ever be. I had to break up with her because I don't want to feel like my potential wife settled for me. I want be someone's first choice, even though I'm not the sort of man who tends to inspire strong feelings.

What if I'm hoping for the impossible?

"Fucking hell," I mutter.

Chapter 6

Kim

AT BREAKFAST, I SIT with Iris and Alex, her husband. Max, luckily, isn't present, and you know who else isn't here? Tessa and Malcolm. Heh.

"So?" Iris says. "How was your night? Did catching the bouquet *mean* something?"

"Fuck, no." I drain my first cup of coffee. "The fact that I caught the bouquet was...unfortunate." I tried my best not to catch it. I really did. Someone who wants to get married deserved that honor.

"I hope you at least had a good time after you left the reception?"

I look at Alex, whom I don't know all that well. He starts to get up.

"No, it's fine," I say. "You can stay. Last night didn't meet my expectations, let's just say that."

Iris is immediately alarmed. "What happened? Did he—"

"I wasn't in any danger," I assure her. "He just wasn't great in bed, but don't tell anyone, okay?"

Iris mimes zipping her lips.

After breakfast, I finish packing up, check out, and start the long drive back to Toronto.

One wedding down, three to go.

I might not want to get married myself, but some people do seem to enjoy marriage. I admit I find it baffling, but there it is. And weddings themselves can be kind of fun. Dancing, food, friends you haven't seen in a while...

I didn't go to any weddings for two years because of the pandemic, and I only had one wedding last year. I missed it a little, truth be told, although three more weddings in less than three months seems like a bit much. Especially since my parents are going to be at all of them.

Yep, I just wasted my best chance to hook up at a wedding on Max.

I heard him leave in the middle of the night; I was just pretending to be asleep because I didn't want to talk to him. To his credit, I don't think he's under any delusions that last night was good for me. I suspect that's why he snuck out and didn't leave a note.

The sex wasn't the worst I've had, but it was over so quickly and I didn't feel satisfied. I thought he'd care more about my pleasure rather than falling asleep two seconds after coming. Instead, I used my vibrator—I often travel with my rabbit vibrator—and gave myself an orgasm this morning.

I'm usually good at picking out hot men who will give me what I want in bed, but last night, I failed.

I seem to be off my game.

The following Saturday, I have dinner with my family.

"Kim!" my mother shouts as I sit down across from her.

Why is she shouting? It's a small table, and the restaurant isn't as busy as it sometimes is. Is she losing her hearing? Do I need to convince her to go to the doctor?

I don't say any of that. I merely greet her with, "Hi, Mom."

For a few minutes, she focuses on ordering, complaining that the prices have gone up.

She's right; they have. For the first time in, like, four years.

I think the restaurant is entitled to raise their prices every now and then.

Believe it or not, I'm the good daughter. Sure, I sleep around—my mom would freak out if she knew—but I have a respectable profession, and I stayed in Toronto, which means I can see my family every month.

Still, you wouldn't know it from the way my parents complain. Lately, it's about the fact that I'm not married and at thirty-two, I'm getting old. My mother keeps sending me articles about how pregnancy becomes harder and riskier with age.

"You're losing weight," she complains.

"I'm not," I say.

Last month, she complained that I was gaining weight, but my weight has stayed exactly the same. The only consistent thing is that it's never right in her eyes.

But if she thinks I'm losing weight, maybe she'll try to heap extra food on my plate. My mom might grumble about the prices, but the food here *is* good. Some of the online reviewers don't approve of the service—the servers aren't smiling and cheerful—but who needs that?

Back in the day, I had a job at one of those generic chain restaurants, and my manager said I wasn't perky enough. Yes, he actually used the word "perky." I would have told him off, but I needed that job.

I do have a sibling, but Freddie isn't here tonight, on account of the fact that he lives in B.C. He dropped out of university many years ago to become a snowboard instructor, and he smokes a lot of weed.

This, of course, was not the path that my parents had planned for him. He didn't meet their expectations, so now they've heaped their expectations on *me*.

Yet he's still the favorite, even if visits only once a year—and never at Christmas or Lunar New Year, because of aforementioned snowboarding. He's the boy, after all.

Occasionally, I consider moving out of Toronto, like Freddie, and seeing my parents only once or twice a year. But then I'd be using my vacation time to visit family, and I don't particularly want to do that, either.

"How was the wedding?" Dad asks after we've placed our orders.

"Good," I say. "Everything went smoothly." I don't mention the shenanigans with the flower girl, nor the fact that it was too cold to fully enjoy an outdoor wedding. And, of course, I don't mention Max.

"She should have had the reception at a Chinese banquet hall." Mom clucks her tongue. "Her mother is Chinese, yes?"

"Tessa wanted to get married in her hometown. No opportunities for a ten-course banquet there."

I admit such food would have been preferable, but I can satisfy my cravings at Isobel's and Carl's weddings.

"Freddie has a girlfriend," Mom says. "Did he tell you?"

No, he did not.

It's been many, many years since my brother mentioned a girlfriend, and I can't help wondering if he really is in a relationship. Did he make it up to please our parents?

No, that sounds ridiculous, but the possibility won't leave my mind. It's easier to get away with such lies when you live on the other side of the country, and even if Mom and Dad discovered the truth, they'd make excuses about him being under so much pressure or similar.

Whereas I still can't live down that time I got a B in grade eight.

Anyway, it's fine. I can manage my family once a month, but the last thing I need is another family to deal with, which is why I'm not getting married.

One thing I will say for my brother: even though he's the favored son, he doesn't get our mother to fight his battles for him, unlike Troy.

I shudder at the memory.

"Are you cold?" Dad asks.

"It's because you're losing weight," Mom says. "It's warm today."

"The air conditioning's a little high," I murmur, sipping my tea.

Mom returns to talking about Freddie. "I hope he'll bring his girlfriend when he visits next month. Maybe you'll have a boyfriend by then, too? You didn't say you're bringing a plus one to Mirabel's wedding, but I'm sure if you change your mind, she could make adjustments."

"I RSVP'd for one. I'm not changing anything."

"You're getting old, Kim. Why don't you go on dates? Did you see that article I sent you yesterday—"

"Yes, Mom. Just like I saw the one you sent three days ago."

She doesn't comment on my snarky tone, perhaps because the waiter is quietly setting a platter of noodles on the table. When he walks away, my mom complains about the amount of shrimp. She thinks there aren't enough, even though the dish is exactly the same as usual.

I briefly wonder what Max's family is like—does his mom delight in complaining?

I shake my head. Enough thinking about Max.

After all, it's not like I'll ever see him again.

Chapter 7

Max

"Max." My mother gives me the smallest of smiles as I take a seat next to her at the restaurant. She's never been prone to expressing good cheer—I take after her more than my father. A slight smile doesn't mean she isn't happy to see me; it's just her way.

Jon sits down on my other side and slaps my back. The baby of the family, he's now twenty-eight. Next to Jon is Leo, then Evan. At thirty-two, Evan is the closest in age to me.

My dad reaches for the teapot. "I thought you were bringing Graham?" he says to Evan.

Evan shakes his head. "We broke up."

"I'm sorry," Dad says.

"Before you ask, Mom, no, he didn't hurt me. Just didn't work out. No need to threaten him with the hedge trimmer."

Mom hasn't explicitly threatened anyone with the hedge trimmer before, but back in high school, Leo's girlfriend left him and immediately started dating his best friend. (I suspect there was some overlap, and I'm sure he does do, but I keep this thought to myself.) When his so-called best friend appeared at the house to try to patch things up, Mom was out in the yard, getting ready to trim the bushes and hedge. Leo's friend asked to speak to him, and Mom just turned on the hedge trimmer and ignored his request. She wasn't very close to him, probably a good three or four meters away.

I know this is what happened because Evan and I were there, trying to fix the lawn mower, but ever since, it's become something of a joke.

Mom never protests and says she wasn't threatening him. No, I think she enjoys the image, truth be told.

"Well, you know what that means." Jon slings his arms around me and Leo. "We're all single for Mirabel's wedding."

Dear God. He's going to tell us that weddings are a great—

"Weddings are a great place to pick up," he says.

As expected.

"I'm not in the mood for that," Evan says.

"That's okay." Jon says cheerfully. "You can just watch Max embarrass himself."

My youngest brother is clearly in one of his annoying moods today, as he is about ninety percent of the time.

Evan smiles. "Sounds like a plan."

Leo says nothing, just smirks.

This is getting out of hand.

"I don't want you to embarrass yourself *too* much," Jon says. "I'll give you pointers."

I open my mouth, then hastily close it. I was about to mention that I successfully picked someone up at last weekend's wedding, but of course it would be foolish to say that out loud.

I've thought far too much about Kim in the past week. About what I'd do if given the chance to redeem myself. About how I'd go down on her until she screamed, then do it again.

But truth be told, I don't actually want the chance to redeem myself. If I did meet Kim in person again, it would be the stuff of nightmares. I'd probably spontaneously combust from shame, so it's best we don't meet again—I don't want my family to have to deal with my untimely demise. My mom isn't the most affectionate person, but she'd take my death particularly hard.

Jon elbows me. "Are you silent because you *did* embarrass yourself last weekend?"

"No," I say shortly. "And I don't need pointers."

"I've never seen you flirt with anyone. I'm not sure you know how."

"I do not flirt with people in your presence. That's why."

"You seem crankier than usual," Evan says. "Is something wrong, Max?"

"Nothing's wrong," I say, but I fear that's not convincing.

Unfortunately, my dad now looks concerned, too.

"If you need help," he says, "I can ask around. Find some eligible young women to introduce you to. What are you looking for? Marriage? A little fling? Personally, I'd recommend marriage." He glances at my mother and smiles. "But—"

"I don't need help from my parents," I tell him.

"Don't bring me into this," Mom says. "This is all on your father. You know I stay out of these things."

"You stay out of them until you threaten someone with a hedge trimmer," Jon says.

Mom responds with a shrug, and Dad laughs.

Just a regular day in the family.

When our food begins to arrive, Mom immediately reaches for the siu mai and winces. It's faint, but it doesn't escape my notice.

"Is something wrong?" I ask. Between my parents, my mother is the stoic one, and it's rare for her to show even the slightest expression of pain.

"I pulled something when I was working in the garden," she says. "Don't worry."

The problem is that I'm a bit of a worrier, even if I don't always say anything, and I've been worrying about my mother since I was seven. When Jon was born, something wasn't right. I'm not actually sure what happened to her—we never talk about it—but she wasn't well for a long time, and she had four little boys to look after. She rarely complained, but I could tell.

I decided I'd do my best not to cause her any stress. Okay, that isn't exactly how I framed it in my seven-year-old mind, but I was determined to be good. I wouldn't get in trouble. I would try to be helpful.

I would be the one she didn't have to worry about.

Mom has always made it clear that she wouldn't put pressure on us to get married, unlike Auntie Gladys with her kids, but I do wonder if that's what she'd like to see. For a split second, I resolve to be more proactive about it. I can enlist Dad's help, sign up for every dating app, and—

No. Mom would never expect me to subject myself to such horrors on her behalf.

But one day, it would be nice to get married, and if I find a woman who can love me like I love her, I hope I make a better first impression than I did on Kim.

My father is the middle child. He has a younger sister, Doreen, as well as an older brother, Gilbert, who is married to Gladys, aka my mother's nemesis. They're only rivals in my aunt's eyes, however; Mom merely thinks Gladys is annoying and overbearing. Not that Mom has said that, precisely, but it's fairly clear what she thinks, and I tend to agree with her.

I presume Auntie Gladys sees my mom as competition because my father's mother—now deceased—was pleased that my mom gave her four grandsons. Gladys has never forgiven Mom for that.

But now, my aunt is "winning" because her kids will all get married before me and my brothers do. Today, it's her eldest daughter's turn.

The wedding is at a lavender farm a little outside of Toronto. Just under an hour from my apartment—if there's no traffic—but I figured it would be easier to stay overnight, so I parked at the hotel before heading over in the shuttle that Dylan's family arranged.

Dylan's family is *very rich*, a fact that has been emphasized by Auntie Gladys an excruciating number of times. If it weren't for that, I'm not sure how thrilled she'd be about Mirabel marrying a white guy, but she's happy with him.

The ceremony won't start for another twenty minutes, but I've already taken my seat. Mom and Gladys are standing to the side of the outdoor seating area, and I can't help overhearing their conversation. They're not that close to me, but my aunt's voice carries.

"Three children getting married in two months!" Gladys says. "Aren't we lucky?" She doesn't give my mother a chance to answer before barreling onward. "I *know* it must sound like a lot, but I really am pleased! My mother is visiting for the entire summer so she can attend all three—isn't that wonderful? It's been *so* much work, though. I swear I've spent a thousand hours on flowers alone."

I imagine my mother is inwardly rolling her eyes at the hyperbole.

"Aiyah!" Gladys says, rushing up to the altar. "No, no, this is all wrong." She yells at someone, who comes over and makes minor adjustments to the arch under which Mirabel and Dylan will be married. Frankly, the "before" and "after" look the same to me.

I'm irritable today because I'm roasting in my suit. It's much warmer for this Canada Day wedding than it was for Malcolm and Tessa's wedding last month. Kim probably would have preferred...

I shut that thought down quickly.

"I'm boiling," Jon complains from my right.

"Yeah, it's very hot," Evan agrees.

Leo, on my left, merely grunts.

"Ooh, who's that?" Jon inclines his head toward a white woman in a pale blue dress.

"Dylan's cousin, I believe," says Evan, who's always been better at keeping track of names and faces than the rest of us. "She was at the engagement party last summer."

Honestly, it's incredible he remembers that.

I study the program before glancing up at Mom and Gladys again, just as Dad joins them, having finished his conversation with some other relative.

"Sorry, I've got to steal my wife away for a moment," he says jovially, taking my mother's arm. I suspect he has no immediate need of my mother, just wants to give her an excuse to get out of that conversation.

As I look around at the people milling about the lavender fields, the back of a woman in a peach dress catches my eyes. She turns slightly, and for a split second, I think it's Kim.

Nah, I must be imagining things. Why would Kim be at my cousin's wedding?

"Looking for someone?" Evan asks.

"Just Aaron and Rory," I lie. Auntie Doreen's sons aren't terribly good at punctuality. I'm not surprised I haven't seen them yet.

As four o'clock approaches, everyone takes their seats. The groom and groomsmen are already standing at the front as the bridesmaids begin walking in. One is Isobel, Mirabel's sister, and another is Dylan's sister; the remaining three are friends.

Then everyone rises in preparation for the bride's entrance. Unlike at Malcolm and Tessa's wedding, I don't get distracted by a pretty bridesmaid, and I stand at the same time as everyone else.

Mirabel enters on the arm of her father. As she walks down the aisle, I keep thinking about how much her dress cost. Perhaps it's unkind of me, but Auntie Gladys has mentioned it a *lot*. It really is a pretty dress, though—not that I know a great deal about such things, but it does look good, and it has an impressive train. I'm sure the pictures, surrounded by fields of lavender, will be stunning.

There's a bit of rustling as everyone sits down, followed by some louder noises. I glance back to see Aaron and Rory strolling in, unbothered by the fact that they're late to their cousin's nuptials, and my gaze lingers on the woman in the peach dress again. She's sitting two rows from the back and...

I turn to face the front as the minister begins speaking. This is Mirabel's wedding, after all; I should pay attention. But I swear...

I can't resist sneaking another look.

Yep, that's definitely Kim.

Chapter 8

Kim

For fuck's sake.

What is Max doing at Mirabel's wedding?

After he snuck out of my room, I figured I'd never see him again, yet here he is, less than a month later, at another wedding. When he notices me, he looks slightly stricken, which is rather satisfying.

Of course, I won't tell him that.

The ceremony isn't long. Once it's over, the newlyweds make their way up the aisle, and I get to my feet.

"Who are they?" I ask my mother casually.

"Who are you talking about? Kim, you have to be clearer."

I don't want to point. "The four men three rows from the front. Are they brothers?"

"Ah. Gilbert's brother's sons. Why? Are you—"

"No," I say shortly. "Just wondering."

I realize, in horror, what this means. Max is Max *Mok*. If he's Mirabel's cousin, then he's also Isobel and Carl's cousin, and he'll almost certainly be at the other two weddings I have to attend this summer. With my parents.

I snort. Just my fucking luck.

"Aiyah!" Mom says. "What was that noise? Is something wrong? You need to make a good impression!"

"I'm fine," I murmur.

The guy from my crappy one-night stand is at this wedding, but otherwise, I'm fine.

There are a hundred and fifty guests. Odds are we won't be seated at the same table for dinner, and from the little I know of Max, I can't imagine he'll tell other people what happened.

Look at me, searching for silver linings.

"You know," Mom says, "a wedding is a great place to meet people."

Yeah, for a fuck.

Obviously, that's not what she means.

"You're thirty-two—"

"If you say anything about my shriveled eggs," I mutter, "I'll scream."

Mom clucks her tongue. "You need to try harder. Remember the time you got a B in grade eight English because you didn't put in the effort? Don't let that happen again."

"Fine," I huff, not in the mood to argue.

She fans herself. "It's too hot today. They should have planned the weather better."

Seriously?

"They booked it more than a year in advance," I say, "and it's not like they can control the forecast. Besides, lavender season isn't that long. I think it only started last weekend."

"It was more comfortable last Saturday."

"Which they couldn't have known fourteen months ago."

"When you get married"—I don't bother correcting her—"I'll make sure the weather is perfect."

"How will you do that?" I ask.

"Ah, why are you arguing with me? It's a beautiful day! We're at a wedding."

"You *just* said it was too hot."

We shuffle forward, waiting to pay our respects to the happy couple and their families in the receiving line. Ten minutes pass before it's finally our turn, and Mom seems determined to have a five-minute conversation with Gladys to make up for the wait, much to the frustration of everyone else behind us—and me.

"Don't worry." Gladys pats my mother's hand. "I'm sure it'll be your turn soon." She shoots me a smile.

I cringe at the thought of marriage, but I try not to let it show.

"Your special man is out there somewhere. Maybe he's even at this wedding." Gladys turns back to my mother. "You must join us for the first round of family photos. Don't say you're not family."

Mom puts up a protest, but I know she's secretly pleased—whereas I'm anything but. I want to be drinking something cold, not standing around in a sunny field.

Oh, and Max is family. There's also that.

Fifteen minutes later, I'm as miserable as expected, surrounded by lots of yelling aunties. Two of them switch places yet again, and the photographer sighs. I hope she's getting paid well for this nightmare.

I've realized why Gladys wants us to be in the family pictures. Dylan's father is apparently one of six kids, and Dylan has tons of cousins; Gladys doesn't want Mirabel's side of the family to look comparatively small. And it's pretty obvious whose family is whose, since Mirabel's is all Asian, and Dylan's is ninety percent white. The photographer has taken a picture of the happy couple with Dylan's family, and we're now preparing for the photo of both families.

I feel someone's hands on me. "You go over here," Gladys says. "You're shorter than Evan. Looks better this way."

I smile briefly at Evan—he's one of Max's brothers, isn't he? He seems to have a sunnier disposition than Max.

"How are you related?" he asks.

"I'm not," I say.

My mom thumps the left side of her chest. "We're related here!"

"That's my mom," I tell Evan. "Our families are friends. We..."

My words trail off as I'm manhandled, yet again, by Gladys, who now has me standing next to Max.

Great.

I glance toward the photographer. Her assistant, a young man wearing all black, is snapping candid shots. Looks like he's taking one of me and Max. Hopefully it's such an ugly photo that nobody will ever see it.

"Stand closer to Kim," my mother says to Max, putting her hands on his arms and shifting him toward me.

He practically recoils from her touch. Is that because he's horrified at the thought of standing so close to me?

I'm admittedly a bit horrified, too. My sex life and my family should be kept far, far apart. I'm half afraid someone will figure out what happened based on our behavior—especially his.

Just then, a little boy hurries toward Max and affixes himself to Max's leg.

Does Max have a kid? For some reason, I wasn't expecting that.

"Nolan," Isobel says, "come back here!"

Ah. The little boy is Daisy and Isobel's son.

"No!" Nolan says. "Uncle Max is my favorite."

Max raises an eyebrow. This appears to be news to him.

"Yeah?" Isobel says. "Why is that?"

Nolan frowns and thinks for a moment. "I don't know, but he is."

I chuckle.

Okay, maybe seeing Max isn't as bad as I initially thought. His reactions are providing some entertainment, distracting me from the fact that I'm baking in the sunshine.

"Why are you laughing, Kim?" Mom demands.

Oh, geez.

"No reason. Just in a good mood."

Max turns to me and raises that eyebrow again. He's only a few inches away and...damn. Why am I still attracted to him after our disastrous night together?

I blame it on the suit. I've always been a sucker for men in suits.

Except there are lots of men in suits here, and he's the one my eye is drawn to. It's a different suit from what he wore last time; that one was dark gray, and this one is light gray, and why am I notice these things? Why am I noticing how the jacket stretches across his broad shoulders as he bends down to pick up Nolan? He hands the boy over to Isobel.

You're an idiot, Kim. You slept with him already, and it didn't go well.

I need some liquor right now. Unfortunately, that will have to wait until we finally finish these family pictures.

"Carl!" Gladys yells. "Move to your left."

"No—" the photographer begins.

I feel like a photographer ought to have better control over a group than she does, but I suspect most families are easier to wrangle.

Finally, she manages to get a few pictures. Then Dylan's family steps aside so Mirabel's family, which apparently includes me, can be photographed alone with the happy couple.

This time, it only takes three minutes for us to arrange ourselves, and it's not long before extended family is free to leave.

Thank God. Time to pour alcohol down my throat.

For my first drink, I try the signature cocktail, which is a mistake.

Since the wedding ceremony and reception are at a lavender farm, someone apparently thought a cocktail involving lavender would be cool or clever or some such nonsense.

Instead, it tastes like body lotion.

And I haven't ingested body lotion since I was Nolan's age.

When I'm ready for a second drink, I look around the patio, searching for one of the servers with glasses of wine, and instead, my gaze lands on Max yet again. Why does that keep happening?

To my amusement, he quickly looks away.

I turn back to Yvonne. "How's the wedding planning?"

This is my first time meeting Yvonne. She's Carl's fiancée, and they're getting married at the end of the summer. I wasn't particularly keen to talk to her—Carl is kind of an ass, so I was afraid the same would be true of her—but she's pleasant. I'm happy to keep her company as I avoid my mother.

"It's..." She sighs, sounding weary to the bone. "I'll be glad when it's over."

"You planning a honeymoon?"

She nods. "Finger Lakes."

A server walks by, and I snag a glass of white wine and have a sip. Yep, definitely better than that cocktail.

I murmur my thanks before returning to my conversation with Yvonne. "I've never been. Upstate New York, right?"

"Yeah. It's been more fun to plan than the wedding."

"Because you don't need to please your family?"

She chuckles. "Perhaps. I—"

"Yvonne!" someone shouts.

I turn and see Carl, stumbling with a glass of wine in each hand.

Her lips thin, just a little, before she pastes on a smile. "It was nice to meet you, Kim, but I better get going. Talk to you later."

As she walks away, I spot Max again. He attempts to duck behind a potted shrub, but he's far too big for that to be successful.

Nolan runs over to him. "Are you playing hide and seek? I want to play!"

I stifle a laugh.

I hadn't planned to talk to Max Mok, but with the lengths he's taking to avoid me, I've changed my mind.

I don't want to make him squirm *too* much, but a little conversation could be fun.

Chapter 9

Max

DINNER SHOULD BE STARTING in a few minutes. Leo, Evan, and I have taken our assigned seats, at Table 3 under a big tent. Mom and Dad are talking with Auntie Doreen, and Jon is flirting with Dylan's cousin. I can't imagine trying to pick up a woman when my parents are within fifty meters of me, but Jon isn't bothered by such things. He leans in and whispers something in her ear, and she appears to be charmed, laughing and touching his arm.

Disturbingly, I'm envious of my brother. Not because I have any interest in Dylan's cousin, but because Jon probably wouldn't have a disastrous one-night stand like I had with Kim.

He swaggers over to the table and sits down beside me.

"That's Mom's seat," I say.

"I know." He lifts up the placard with her name, then puts it down. "But I want to talk to you before she gets here." He slaps my shoulder. "Who's that woman you keep looking at?"

"I don't know what you're talking about." I try not to show how alarmed I am that he noticed, but my hand shakes as I reach for my water glass.

"Do you mean the woman in the peach dress?" Evan asks Jon, who nods in response. "I noticed that, too. Who is she?"

"Kim," I grunt, then realize my error. I just admitted to knowing her name.

"Now this is interesting," Jon says, in that annoying way little brothers have. You know, the way that makes you want to throttle them.

"Not interesting," I say. "I heard Auntie Gladys call her that."

He points at me. "You're lying."

"Why would I lie?"

Evan leans toward us. "I think Jon's right. Something's going on. You keep looking at her, then looking away as soon as she sees you. I even saw you hiding behind a shrub at one point."

Jon doubles over in laughter. Bastard.

"It looked ridiculous," Evan says, "and that's not how you'd act with someone you just met today."

Leo nods.

Jon keeps laughing.

I'm not sure why my parents felt the need to give me three younger brothers. It was truly unnecessary.

"Do you have history?" Jon asks.

"No," I say shortly, but I'm starting to doubt my *deny, deny, deny* strategy. I don't think my brothers are buying it.

Jon turns to Evan. "Do you believe him?"

"Of course not," Evan says.

"What about you?" Jon asks Leo.

"No," Leo grunts.

I shoot him a glare, but he's distracted by something on the other side of the tent.

"Has she turned you down, Max?" Jon asks in singsong voice that he knows I hate.

"No."

"Interesting. Very interesting." He strokes his nonexistent beard before snapping his fingers. "I know. You spent the night together, but your performance left something to be desired."

Sometimes, unfortunately, Jon guesses the truth, and I can tell by the look on his face that he knows he's hit upon it.

No point in denial now.

"Before you jump to more conclusions," I say, desperately wishing a server would come around with some wine, "I didn't treat her badly. It just could have gone better."

Evan nods sympathetically.

"What could have gone better?" Dad asks.

Shit. I didn't notice my parents approaching the table.

"Nothing," I say.

"Actually…" Jon begins.

I'm pretty sure he's not going to tell my parents what we were talking about. He's just doing his best to get on my nerves.

At least, I think that's the case.

"You're in my seat." Mom taps Jon on the shoulder.

I relax a little once I have my mother beside me rather than my youngest brother, but then something knocks into me, and I nearly fall off my chair.

"Max!" Nolan says. "I found you."

This is the other part of today that I don't know how to deal with: the fact that Isobel and Daisy's son has decided I'm his favorite.

I have no idea why. Honestly, none.

I don't dislike kids, but I wouldn't say I'm great with them; Evan's the one who babysat as a teenager. I'm completely baffled by what Nolan sees in me.

However, there's something nice about being a child's favorite, even if said child is in the process of grabbing your pants with his sticky hands.

"It's my turn to hide!" he exclaims.

Apparently, we're still playing hide and seek.

"I think it's dinner time," I say. The emcee—one of Dylan's friends—is adjusting the microphone. "I'll take you back to your mother, okay?"

Nolan doesn't seem impressed with this idea, but he allows me to take his hand and guide him toward Daisy, who's only a few steps away.

When I turn around, I notice a flash of peach out of the corner of my eye.

Why can't I stop noticing her? Why?

Worst of all, my brothers now have some idea of what happened, and that will make it even harder to behave sensibly in front of her. At least I can take comfort in the fact that she hasn't seemed particularly interested in speaking to me, either.

I hope that will continue.

After dinner and dessert, the dancing begins. I have no interest in partaking in such activities, and my head feels a little odd, perhaps from all the wine I consumed to chase away the memory of what happened with Kim. As I exit the tent, I see her looking at a large collage of the happy couple, a smile on her face. For a split second, I'm convinced it's a sign that she secretly wants romance. A relationship.

Then I shake my head. I hardly know her.

And why would I care anyway?

I walk over to the wooden fence lining the patio, separating it from the lavender, and look out at the fields. It's still warm and humid, but the sun has just set, and it's not as oppressively hot as it was earlier.

"Hey."

I haven't heard that voice too many times, but I recognize it all the same.

"Hi, Kim." I turn to look at her. With the lights on the patio, I can still make her out pretty well. This is the closest I've been to her all day. Her dress only exposes a hint of cleavage, but it's mesmerizing all the same.

I should not be thinking of such things. However, the truth is that I've thought about a lot more than that in the past few weeks.

"You've been avoiding me." Her tone is playful.

My heart starts beating faster. I can't believe she actually confronted me.

"In fact," she says, "I even noticed you hiding behind a potted shrub at one point, and you, Max Mok, are a tall man who does not fit behind a potted shrub."

"I was playing hide and seek with Nolan."

"I don't think you were."

Fair. Nolan is the only person who believed we were playing hide and seek.

I look out at the lavender since it's too hard to look at her. "Yes, I was avoiding you. I'm conscious of the fact that the last time we saw each other, my performance left something to be desired."

"Which is why you made your escape just after midnight."

"You were awake when I left?"

"I was."

This is just getting worse and worse, and I didn't think that was possible. It really is a miracle that I haven't combusted from shame.

"I'm sorry—"

"No," she says, "it's probably for the best that you didn't stay."

I'm not sure I can take much more of this.

"Does anyone know about us?" she asks.

"My brothers figured it out. Don't worry, they won't gossip."

"Tell me about your brothers. You're Mirabel's cousins, so I'm told."

I nod. "I'm the oldest. Then Evan, the accountant. Leo, with the shaved head and tattoos, is the artistic one. Jon, the youngest, is a lawyer. He's the most annoying."

She chuckles. "Jon...he was flirting with the white lady in the blue dress?"

"Mm-hmm. He likes to sleep around." I pause. "No judgment. I—"

"Yes, yes, that does describe me. It's fine. Though people treat women who do that differently from men."

"I know. It's not fair."

We're silent for a moment. There's a light breeze, which is refreshing. I've started sweating since Kim joined me.

I'm very aware of her proximity. Her hair is down, unlike at the last wedding, and she's wearing a simple gold necklace.

I wished I hadn't messed things up with her. I do like her. I like that she was bold and took the lead last time. I like that she sought me out tonight, even if it makes me squirm.

Then I remind myself that it doesn't matter. She wants different things from me—as evidenced by the fact that she tried her best not to catch Tessa's bouquet. Sure, she was smiling as she looked at the collage, but I shouldn't read into it. She might see a relationship as something that's good for other people, just not for her.

"I need you to know," I say, "that I can do much better than I did last time." Even though I don't have a chance with her, I can't have her thinking that was my best. "I just...I'm really not good with one-night stands. That was my first—"

"I was your first one-night stand?"

"And last. Clearly, they're not suited to my strengths. I do better when I know the person, know how to read them, know what they like. I...yeah. I was a bit anxious, and I wish..."

It's time to shut up. I've shared more than I should have, and she doesn't need to know all the daydreams I've had about her since. Ones where I made her scream for me again and again.

"You wish what, Max?" She steps closer and knocks her shoulder against my arm.

I shake my head.

"You wish you had a do-over?" she asks. "Tell me, what would you do if you had another chance?"

Chapter 10

Kim

I can't believe I asked that question. Why can't I move on?

When I approached Max outside the tent, I didn't expect to exchange more than a few words with him. He'd done his best to hide from me today, after all. But although he's been looking at the lavender—rather than at me—he's been relatively forthright. There's something appealing about that, even if he didn't rock my world the last time I saw him.

"You don't need to answer," I say hurriedly. "Forget it."

"I'm happy to answer. Unless you don't want me to?"

Why does his voice make my skin tingle? Why is there a pulse between my legs?

I think that's why I can't completely get over this. I'm still affected by him, despite our history, and I'm curious. My curiosity has gotten the better of me.

I gesture for him to continue.

He looks at me for a moment, his dark eyes piercing in the dim light, before turning back to the fields. He rests his arms on the fence.

Music and laughter drift out of the tent. God, I think that's my mother's laugh. What if she comes out here? I'm not doing anything inappropriate with Max—aside from the subject of our conversation—but if she sees us, she might start planning the wedding.

Yet despite the fear of her finding us, I don't leave. I want him to answer.

"I still have some of the problems I had before," he says. "I don't know you very well. I don't know what you like, in bed and elsewhere. When we were together, I'm pretty sure you didn't come—"

"You're correct."

"—although there are some women who don't orgasm, so I've heard—"

"I'm not one of them. Making me come isn't too difficult."

"That makes what happened even more embarrassing."

I hesitate. "I like it a little rough and dirty. I enjoy feeling filthy. And I like being touched everywhere, including my breasts, which you studiously avoided."

He sighs. "My ex was very ticklish there, so—"

"I understand." I don't want to hear about his ex. It shouldn't bother me, but it does.

He says nothing more, and the silence between us feels charged. When he drums his fingers on the fence, the sound seems to echo in my chest. Staying or walking away—it shouldn't be a big deal, but somehow, it is. My feet are rooted to the ground, and when he shifts the tiniest bit toward me, I nearly gasp.

There was something intimate about discussing my needs without actually doing anything. It wasn't sexy, exactly, but definitely intimate, and I have a feeling he won't forget what I said.

I really wish we'd both slowed down that night. Maybe we would have had a good time. And looking at him now in the shadows, handsome and serious, his attention all focused on me...I wonder if this isn't over. I feel an unexpected sense of anticipation.

He brushes my hair back from my face; my lips part of their own accord.

But he doesn't kiss me.

I try not to feel too disappointed.

"Kim," he whispers. "Is it short for Kimberly?"

"Yes." No one calls me that, though.

"If I had another chance, I promise I'd take very, *very* good care of you." He leans down, and I feel his breath on my heated cheeks. My nipples are embarrassingly tight, desperate for his touch. "I would devote myself to your pleasure. I'd have you squirming on my fingers. Writhing against my face. Coming apart on my cock."

Yes. Something about his simple, straightforward tone, the fact that he can't look at me as he speaks, so close yet not touching me...I can hardly stand it. It's too much, and I'm about to combust.

I wish he'd stick his hand up my skirt and feel how wet I am.

I want him to know.

"I'd spank you," he says. "I'd hold you down. Make you come as many times as possible."

Oh, God. I'm picturing it. His stern expression as he smacks my heated flesh. My cries of ecstasy as I twist in the sheets beneath him.

When he speaks again, his voice is even lower. Dangerously slow and seductive, and I don't think he's aware how good he is at this. "I'd utterly wreck you."

Every inch of me is vibrating with need. My pussy clenches. I barely manage to release a shuddering breath.

I want all that. I want him to wreck me. I want to be a sated and giggly mess afterward.

Fucking Max Mok.

I turn to him, tilting my head up instinctively; I don't have full control over my body right now. He leans forward and brushes his lips over my cheek. Just the briefest of touches.

I moan.

"I better go back inside," he says.

And then he's gone.

I return to the tent and try to mingle, but I can't do it. I can't stay here any longer.

Luckily, there's a shuttle at ten thirty, so I say my goodbyes and head to the parking lot, where the van is waiting.

I lean my head against the cool window as we drive toward the hotel in Milton. It's ten minutes away, which seems far too long. My heart is pounding. My pussy is pulsing. I'm a mess.

All thanks to a guy who disappointed me the last time we met.

When the van reaches the hotel, I fly up the stairs to my room, not wanting to wait by the elevator—I'm only on the second floor. As soon as I shut the door behind me and slip off my shoes, I go to my suitcase and pull out my rabbit vibrator. I lean against the wall, tip my head back, and slide it inside me, sighing in relief.

Yes, this is what I need. I'm a horny bitch. I'm meant to be filled.

I manhandle my breasts as I move the toy in and out...and then I turn it on. I adjust the vibration mode to what I want as I continue to play with myself.

I imagine Max squinting in concentration as he studies the toy, as he experiments with what it can do to me. He ramps up the intensity until I'm squirming and gripping the sheets, losing myself in an orgasm. Then he removes the toy, sliding the whole thing in his mouth to suck off my juices, and thrusts his cock inside me. I'm incoherent with pleasure as he pins my hands above my head and takes me with slow, deep strokes. He touches my clit just the way I like it, and I come again, and when he spills himself inside me—no need to use condoms in a fantasy—I shudder in satisfaction.

I thrust the toy furiously, hoping I can feel it tomorrow. I imagine his cum leaking out of me. As I said, I like it filthy. I imagine him going down on me afterward, buttoned-up Max—still wearing his glasses—licking the mess he's made of my pussy.

I scrunch up my eyes and open my mouth in a silent scream before sliding down the wall and collapsing on the floor. The vibration is almost painful against my sensitive clit now, but I don't turn it off. It feels right. He intended to make me come a bunch of times, and so I will.

I shudder again and again until I finally remove the vibrator. Not for the first time, I fall asleep cursing Max.

Chapter 11

Max

A FEW MINUTES LATER, when I'm no longer painfully hard—a long reflection on load-bearing walls did the trick, once I got over the word "load"—I head back into the tent.

My eyes search out Kim; I can't seem to help it. But she's nowhere to be found.

"Your lady friend...she left." Jon comes up to me.

"Thanks for the update."

He gives me a mock salute and disappears.

My parents are dancing to a slow song. Mom has never been much of a dancer, but Dad is, and he usually gets her to dance to one or two songs. More if she's trying to avoid Auntie Gladys.

But since it's her daughter's wedding, Gladys is in high demand. She's currently talking to Mirabel's new mother-in-law. Mirabel is the first of the cousins to get married, even though most of us are in our thirties. I'm the oldest, but given how I've been performing lately, I suppose it's not surprising that I'm still single.

Jesus. I can't believe I said those words to Kim. Dirty talk isn't the sort of thing I do, well, ever. But when she asked what I'd do if given the chance, I couldn't seem to help myself. And I was watching her out of the corner of my eye. She was clearly turned on. I wouldn't have done it if she hadn't been into it.

Though now that it's over, I feel weird about it. We were alone, but not far from the rest of the wedding guests. *My cousin's wedding.*

I head to the bar.

"What can I get you?" the bartender asks.

"Whiskey," I tell her. "On the rocks."

As soon as she hands me the glass, I dump half the alcohol into my mouth. Unfortunately, I also get an ice cube in the process, and I start hacking away.

"What's wrong with Max?" a child's voice asks.

Why is Nolan still up? It must be way past his bedtime.

Daisy ushers him away so I can consume my alcohol and have my coughing fit in peace.

"I'm going to head out and—hey, you okay?" Evan places a hand on my back.

"Yeah, just swallowed an ice cube." I hold up my glass.

My brother frowns. "Are you drinking whiskey? Does this have to do with Kim? You know, everyone has their off nights. It's okay."

Since I can't tell Evan about the conversation I just had, I simply nod. Then I down the rest of the whiskey, careful not to get any ice cubes, and ask for more. Neat, this time.

Evan, who rarely drinks, looks on with concern. "Are you sure you're okay?"

"I'm fine." I know I haven't convinced anyone, not even myself.

"Look, I'm driving Mom and Dad home—you know Mom doesn't like being out too late—so I should get going. But you and Leo are sharing a hotel room, right?"

"Yep."

I'm dimly aware of Evan going over to Leo, who's nursing a glass of liquor and looking at something on his phone. When Evan points in my direction, Leo scowls.

"I'm okay," I say, even though I'm on my way to drunk.

I stumble, but there was a napkin on the floor, I swear. I didn't just trip on my own two feet. Really, I didn't.

"Yo, Max," Aaron says, coming over with a beer in hand. "What's up?" He slaps me on the shoulder and gives me an easy smile.

Rory, as usual, isn't far behind him.

In their mid-twenties, Aaron and Rory are the youngest of my cousins. They like hockey—both watching and playing—and going out for a drink.

"Let's do a shot!" Rory says. "Tequila for us and a special for you. A cement mixer."

I'm not falling for that. "Nope."

"Aw, come on, I thought you liked cement. Aren't you, like—what's it called? A structural engineer?"

"That doesn't mean I like cement...in my mouth."

Aaron bends over, slaps his leg, and laughs, and I find myself laughing along. What is wrong with me?

"What *do* you like in your mouth?" Rory asks.

I think of Kim, of course.

My cousins don't push me to answer, though. That's not their style.

"How about a prairie fire?" Aaron suggests.

"I won't do a shot with hot sauce." But thanks to the booze flowing through my veins, I don't feel too irritated by his suggestion.

He slaps me on the shoulder again. "That's fine. Three tequila shots, coming right up! You enjoying yourself tonight? Cool party, isn't it? All those purple flowers were pretty. They'll look nice in the pics, I bet."

I do a tequila shot with my cousins before they wander off. That's the first shot I've done in many, many years. Then I grab a third glass of whiskey and collapse on the chair next to Leo.

"Hey, bro," I say, patting his arm.

He looks alarmed. "How about we go back to the hotel?"

"No." I cross my arms. "No alcohol there."

"I'm not sure you need more—I can't believe you did a shot—but I do have a bottle of vodka in my suitcase."

I start laughing. Leo has a bottle of alcohol in his suitcase! How hilarious!

He glances at his watch. "The next shuttle's in ten minutes. Can you manage a moving vehicle?"

"I'm not *that* drunk."

"I think you might be, and I'm jealous. It takes a lot more to get me drunk."

Something's up with Leo. He's frowning—wait, no. That doesn't mean anything; he's always frowning. Still, something's different. Like, his frown is frownier than usual.

I let out a sound that might be a hiccup. "Kim doesn't do relationships." But I still have enough wits about me to know that I shouldn't tell him what I said to her.

I'd utterly wreck you.

"Well." Leo pauses. "You're not going to remember this tomorrow, so I can say it."

"Say what?"

"At least she isn't engaged to your cousin."

When I slowly, painfully, become conscious the next morning, the last thing I recall clearly is Leo saying that at least Kim isn't engaged to my cousin. I told myself this was important and I needed to remember it.

I'm pretty sure he meant Yvonne (engaged to Carl), not Daisy (engaged to Isobel). He looked in Yvonne's direction after saying that. I swear he did.

I'm not misremembering, am I?

After that conversation, the night becomes hazy, but I do remember bits and pieces. The shuttle...coming back to the room...Leo's bottle of Smirnoff.

Shit. I haven't gotten that drunk in *years*.

I sit up and instantly regret it. I haven't had a hangover since well before the pandemic. I don't like losing control of myself, even just a little; I can't remember the last time I had more than three drinks in a night.

Deciding that sitting up is too much effort, I slide back down and curl up under the blankets with my eyes closed. That's better. Except there's some really loud shuffling. I open one eye—to expose myself to less light—and see Leo packing up his suitcase. He's dressed in jeans and a T-shirt.

Leo and I don't look much alike, except to people who think all Asians look the same. He's stocky and five inches shorter than me, but his arm muscles are probably twice as big as mine.

"You're awake," he grunts.

"Please. Don't be so loud."

"I was whispering," he says, in what is definitely not a whisper. "I have to get home, but I'm glad to see you're alive. Checkout time is eleven, remember."

I don't like that he's trying to look after me. I'm five years older than him; it should be the other way around.

Something else occurs to me. I'm pretty sure of the answer, but… "Did Mom see me drunk?"

"No, Evan claimed you were in the washroom when they were saying goodbye."

Good. Because me getting wasted would make Mom worry, and I don't need that.

In an attempt to show that I'm not a complete mess, I sit up again, managing not to wince too much.

"I made you some coffee." Leo puts it on the bedside table. "It's pretty weak stuff, so you'll probably want to get something else before you drive back."

"Thanks." I reach for the cup. It takes far more effort than it should. "What did you tell me about Yvonne last night?"

He shoots me a murderous glare, confirming my suspicions.

"But you haven't said anything to her, right?" I want to be clear on what's happening.

"God, no."

We don't speak again as he picks up his suitcase and exits the room. I down my coffee, then have a shower, which makes me feel marginally better but not much. Painkillers should help, though, and I always have a small bottle in my toiletries case.

Except I can't find it.

I look everywhere in my suitcase, but it's nowhere to be found. Shit. Okay, I'll have to find a pharmacy. Then I'll go to Tim Hortons before I begin the drive.

I try not to look too hungover as I head down to the lobby, but then I see *her*.

She's at the front desk, handing over her key card. She's wearing tiny shorts, and it's the first time I've seen her in something other than a dress—or nothing at all. I nearly mutter a curse under my breath, and it's not because I'm hungover.

Okay, Max, don't stare. Last night, you told her you wanted her squirming against your face, but it's no biggie.

Unfortunately, that doesn't help.

However, something occurs to me: she might have Tylenol, and my desire to calm the throbbing in my head wins out over my desire to hide behind the group of people who have just entered the lobby.

When she turns around and heads for the exit, I say, "Hi, Kim."

Chapter 12

Kim

WHEN MAX MOK SAYS hello to me, I feel myself blush, which pisses the shit out of me. I'm a modern woman, comfortable with my sexual side. I do not blush over a mere "hello."

Except my body seems to come alive at the sound of his voice.

"Hi, Max." I hope I sound normal.

I'm used to seeing him in a suit, but now he's wearing a polo shirt and khaki shorts.

Max in *shorts*. It seems all wrong. Nearly as wrong as him wearing, I don't know, an inflatable T-Rex costume.

His brows pinch together. "Do you have any painkillers?"

Ah. Is that the only reason he spoke to me rather than hiding?

"I do." I reach into my purse and pull out a small bottle. "Take whatever you need."

He dumps two into his hand and swallows them dry.

Does he have a hangover? Huh. It seems wrong for him to be hungover, just like it seems wrong for him to be wearing shorts. I feel like I'm in some alternate reality.

Perhaps that explains the next words out of my mouth. "I'm going to Tim Hortons now. Want to come with me? It's practically next door."

He nods, and after he hands over his key card to the front desk, we head outside. He winces at the sunshine but doesn't say anything as we put our stuff in our cars.

Yep, he's hungover.

Truly bizarre. He must have had a lot more to drink after I left—he didn't seem drunk when we were talking. Or perhaps he was? Perhaps that's the reason he answered my question.

Tell me, what would you do if you had another chance?

My inner muscles clench at the memory of how I hurried to my hotel room and fucked myself hard.

God, things with Max have been so weird.

But going to Tim Hortons together? That's pretty normal. I order a medium coffee and a Boston cream donut, though I regret my order as soon as I say it out loud. "Cream" makes me think of...

Yeah, I've always had a dirty mind.

Max orders a breakfast sandwich, a bottle of water, and a large coffee. I'm amused that it's a double-double. I'm not sure why, but I half expected him to be the sort of guy who takes his coffee black. Maybe he's just having cream and sugar because of his hangover.

We sit down, and there's an awkward silence. I can *feel* the words he said between us, even if neither of us mentions them.

I bite into my donut and get some chocolate on my lip. When I swipe it off with my finger, his expression doesn't change, but his gaze zeroes in on my mouth. My skin tingles.

"Any plans for the day?" I ask.

"Laundry. Preparing my lunches for the week."

He's one of those meal-prep people. I shouldn't be surprised. I picture him at his kitchen counter with an array of containers in front of him, and for some reason, I smile.

"I should do some laundry, too," I say. "Eat something more nutritious than a donut." I hold up said donut. "Probably also field a phone call from my mom, who will want to discuss the wedding in excruciating detail."

"You have my condolences."

"Thank you. Also, the air conditioning in my car is broken, so I'll need to cool off once I get home. Hopefully the drive won't be too long."

He nods before biting into his sandwich. He still looks a little worse for wear.

Okay, I have to ask. "How much did you drink?"

"Too much."

I can't help laughing, but I stop myself from asking why he got drunk, which I'm positive is out of character for him. Does it have something to do with me?

We're having a "normal" conversation, but it's punctuated by loaded silences.

"You'll be at Isobel's and Carl's weddings, I assume?" he asks.

Now it's my turn to nod before taking another bite of my donut.

He sips his coffee. "Can I ask you something?"

"Ask away, but I can't guarantee I'll answer."

"Fair." He pauses. "Why don't you do relationships? Why were you so terrified of catching Tessa's bouquet? You said it was a stupid tradition, but that doesn't explain..."

"To be clear, I don't believe catching the bouquet *means* anything. I was just keen to avoid everyone's comments."

"Understandable."

"And I used to date, but my ex..."

"What did he do?" There's an edge to Max's quiet voice. Foolishly, I rather like it.

I swallow. "When you're in a serious relationship, the other person's family is part of the deal, and I can't overstate how much I hate that. Troy's mother was always making little digs at me. Clearly, she didn't think I was good enough for her son, but trust me, it was the other way."

"I'm sure it was." There's no sarcasm in Max's voice. "He should have stood up for you."

"Ha! He ran to his mama whenever we had problems. Then she'd call me and yell at me. I know she would have been the mother-in-law from hell, and there are lots of in-laws from hell out there."

"My...never mind." Max shakes his head. "Did you have issues with other exes' families?"

"Yep, I'm working with many data points here. There was also the ex with the racist dad, not to be confused with the ex whose dad had a terrible temper. Then there was the ex whose mom had a key to his apartment and used it at random times, which he failed to tell me. She found us making out on his couch. I was topless, naturally."

"That's horrible."

"Is the thought of me topless that horrible?" I can't resist teasing him.

"Of course not," he grunts, then gulps his coffee.

"One of my exes had divorced parents, so we had to do Christmas three times—once with my family, once with each of his parents. I broke up with him before Lunar New Year, since I couldn't stand the thought of doing that again. Tessa said that if I really cared for someone—and his mother didn't keep insulting me to my face—then it wouldn't feel like a burden. But it's always felt like a burden to me. I gave relationships a serious chance, and now, I've moved on. I'm in my slut era."

Max nearly spits out his coffee.

I admit I said that partly to get a reaction, though I half expect him to say I shouldn't call myself a slut.

He doesn't. Perhaps he can tell that I'm not putting myself down. No, even if I haven't had as much sex as I like lately, I'm glorying in being a fun-loving, sexual being.

To emphasize this, I pull down the neckline of my shirt, just a little.

He looks, then he turns to gaze out the window, as if pretending he didn't notice.

Heh.

"I still can't believe," I say, "that I saw you at the next wedding I attended, and I'll see you at two more. Weddings with our entire families. Though I shouldn't be surprised—it's just the sort of thing that would happen to me. You know, to go along with my ex's mom finding me topless."

Hmm. I do enjoy Max's company, even when he's not saying naughty things. He really listens to what you say—and, okay, I enjoy the casual look on him, too. That blue polo shirt somehow manages to be the perfect color on him, although perhaps any shade of blue would look good on Max.

Some colors, however, I don't think he could pull off. Neon green, for example. Bright pink. Bright yellow. I think he'd look thoroughly uncomfortable in those colors, and I chuckle at the image.

He raises his eyebrows but doesn't ask why I'm laughing. I kind of love his slight facial expressions.

"I'm just imagining you wearing a neon green shirt," I explain.

"May I ask why?"

I shrug. "No idea. But I'm sure you'd hate it."

"You would be correct."

All of a sudden, I'm overcome with a pang of longing. To have more quiet mornings like this with Max. I'd say a ridiculous thing here and there—sometimes I lack a filter—and he'd arch an eyebrow and touch my leg...

I wish I'd met him before I gave up on relationships.

What a foolish thought.

I shift in my chair, and oh God, I can feel that I fucked myself good and hard because of *him*.

I shove the last bite of donut into my mouth. "It was great chatting with you, Max." I don't sound like myself. "I better get going."

Back in the parking lot of the hotel, I see Jon swagger out the door with Dylan's cousin. They're laughing.

When I first met Max, I just wanted a simple, hot one-night stand—like the kind those two probably enjoyed—and now I'm wishing I was interested in relationships again, for the first time in years. That man has me all mixed up.

He should have stood up for you, Max said.

But would Max Mok actually be different? Like I told him, it wasn't just one bad experience that made me swear off dating; it was a bunch of them. Every single long-term relationship I've had.

As I pull onto the 401, windows rolled down because of my busted a/c, I remind myself that I don't want to bend and shrink myself to what some man and his family want. I've never benefited, emotionally, from a relationship; they've always come at a cost for me, at least beyond the first few months. Honestly, the main things relationships have given me are regular sex and someone to reach food on high shelves.

It's silly to do something again and again, expecting it to yield it different results, when it's always done the same thing in the past. Yet I did that for years because I thought a romantic relationship could fulfill me. Because some part of me longed for that kind of connection.

The other day, I read an article about women being happier than men after divorce, which didn't surprise me one bit. I'm glad I figured that shit out before I shackled myself to a guy.

Nope, Max is dangerous and I shouldn't get involved.

But despite myself, I smile at the thought of seeing him at the next wedding.

Chapter 13

Max

When Malcolm texted me and asked if I wanted to grab a drink, I suggested we have lunch instead. Alcohol has lost its appeal after Mirabel and Dylan's wedding.

So, the following Saturday afternoon, we meet at a patio for fried chicken and mac and cheese au gratin. Malcolm also orders a dark 'n stormy, but I stick with water.

Once he's finished regaling me with stories about his honeymoon in France, he says, "You've been quieter than normal. Anything new?"

"Not much," I say. "Work. The usual."

"You had another wedding to go to, didn't you?"

"My cousin's." I don't feel like adding more.

Malcolm leans forward. "I heard a little rumor that you left with Kim Sung at our wedding?"

I tense when I hear her name. "We did not leave together."

"But you were seen exiting her room just after midnight."

I wonder which busybody I have to thank for that. Probably Bryce.

Some men might talk about their sex lives with their friends, but not me. My private life is generally...private. But since I don't think I can deny it, I say, "Uh. Yeah. That happened."

"Have you seen her since then?"

"She's family friends with my cousin."

"You mean she was at the wedding this past weekend?"

"Yes."

Malcolm sets down his piece of chicken and laughs. I glare at him.

"And?" He gestures for me to continue.

"And nothing. We saw each other again, that's all."

"So you're not dating. You just had a one-night stand."

"Correct."

"I never thought I'd see the day that you, Max Mok—"

"I know my own name, thank you," I say.

"—had a one-night stand."

I shrug and focus on my mac and cheese, which is deliciously creamy.

"Max?" Malcolm says.

"I'm enjoying my food."

"Nothing else you want to say about Kim?"

"Nope."

"A gentleman doesn't kiss and tell, and you're a gentleman?"

"Something like that." I try not to think about the decidedly ungentlemanly things I said to her—or the things I wanted to do to her when I saw her ass in those shorts.

"I don't expect any details about that night. I'm just surprised." He chuckles. "You and Kim. You're very different people."

I instinctively stiffen, as if expecting him to insult her, even though she's his wife's friend. "Is there a problem with that?"

"No, no, opposites attract and all that, but having opposite views on many things in life...well, it can be a problem."

Yes, exactly.

After we finish our food, Malcolm shows me some wedding pictures on his phone. As I look at the happy photos of Tessa and Malcolm, I also remember the framed photo of my parents on their wedding day, the one that hangs in their bedroom.

I murmur my appreciation, but inside, I feel a twinge of envy.

"Where should I put this, Mom?" I hold up the gift bag that contains ice wine and other goodies for my father's sixty-fifth birthday.

"There's a table out back with all the gifts," she says, gesturing with a spatula.

Through the screen door that leads to the backyard of my childhood home, I can hear Auntie Gladys saying how she would have offered to host her dear brother's birthday but she's just *so* tired with all the wedding planning, and did everyone know that Mirabel's wedding was *only* two weeks ago, and wasn't it lovely?

"Do you need any help in here?" I ask my mother.

"Ah, you know I'm not cooking most of the food myself. Leo should be here with it any minute. Go outside." She shoos me out the back.

"Happy birthday, Dad," I say to my father when I step outside.

He's sitting with Uncle Gilbert and Auntie Gladys at the main table on the patio; Evan and Jon are talking to Aaron and Rory in another corner. Isobel and Daisy are introducing Nolan to the turtle-shaped sandbox, a relic from my childhood that my father dragged out of the basement. Mirabel has been allowed to miss this event for a good reason: she's on her honeymoon. Carl is here but I don't see Yvonne, though maybe she's in the house. There are also a few family friends and one of my dad's friends from work.

It'll be a somewhat exhausting afternoon of socializing, and I saw everyone just two weeks ago, as Gladys so helpfully reminded us. And as I look out at my family, I think of what Kim told me the morning after Mirabel's wedding, about the reason she doesn't do relationships.

I'd wanted to protest and say that my family really isn't so bad and of course I would stand up for her if she were my girlfriend, but it was clear she didn't want to hear it.

I sort of got her point. If my mom weren't married to my dad, I'm positive she'd have nothing to do with Auntie Gladys. Plus, my mom's relationship with her mother-in-law was somewhat strained—as was her relationship with her father-in-law. But I can't imagine my mother not marrying my father because of them.

"What are you sulking about?" Jon tries to shove a bottle of beer into my hand, but I shake my head.

"I'm not *sulking*," I say.

"Could have fooled me."

I look for an escape and happen on Daisy and Nolan, who's flinging sand with a little shovel. I crouch down on the grass next to the sandbox.

"Ready for the big day?" I ask Daisy.

"As ready as I can be," she says.

Nolan looks up from his shoveling and grins. "Max!"

His expression warms my heart. I do like being his favorite.

"You enjoying the sandbox?" I ask.

He nods.

"It used to be mine," I say, "when I was little like you."

Nolan frowns. "Do you want it back?"

"No, you can keep it."

He gives me a hug. "You can have this." He hands me a plastic mold of an alligator, then climbs out of the sandbox with another animal—I think it's a camel? He walks over to Gladys. "Po Po, it's for you."

"Thank you," she coos. "What is it?"

"A droma... A dromedary!"

"You see?" Gladys says to whoever is listening. "He's so smart."

One thing I will say for my aunt: she's not at all bothered by the fact that Nolan isn't, biologically, related to her. Daisy was pregnant with Nolan with she and Isobel got back together, and so Gladys has known him since birth.

When Isobel came out—many years ago now—Gladys wouldn't have considered disowning her lesbian teenage daughter, but she was a little disappointed. She also kept obsessing over what Isobel's potential children, who could have two mothers, would call their grandmas, since the words for maternal and paternal grandmother are different in Chinese and *obviously*, they couldn't both be "maternal grandma." But Nolan only has one grandmother in his life; Daisy isn't on speaking terms with her mother, and Nolan's biological father and his family aren't in the picture.

I look at the plastic alligator in my hand, feeling less special than I did a moment ago, and after chastising myself for that silly thought, I go back inside, slipping off my shoes by the back door. Leo and my mother are putting the food onto serving dishes, so I help them. When it's the three of us, not much needs to be said.

But it's not long before my mom speaks. "I hear you got drunk at Mirabel's wedding?"

Who told her that?

"I misjudged my tolerance," I say. "That's all."

"Hmm."

I hope she's not worried about me, and I hope that nobody said anything to her about me and Kim.

Fortunately, she doesn't say anything more.

Jon comes in and grabs a piece of barbecued duck off the plate. Mom glares at him.

"Is this what you want for your sixty-fifth birthday next year, Mom?" he asks.

"Aiyah!" she says. "You know I don't have this many people in my house if I can help it. You four can come over, but that's all. I'm doing this just for your father."

We set up the food on a table outside, and everyone loads up their own plates. Afterward, there's a birthday cake, no candles, as blowing out candles is something we stopped doing during the pandemic.

As my father opens his gifts, I'm even quieter than I usually am at such things, thinking about how Kim would fit into my family. My mother isn't an amiable, make-everyone-feel-at-home kind of person, but I don't think Kim would mind, and Mom wouldn't insult Kim. If she did, I certainly wouldn't stand for it.

No, I'm convinced my family wouldn't give her the problems she's had in the past, but how can I get Kim to give me a chance?

I'm not sure.

I like that she knows what she wants and what she's worth. She isn't willing to settle, and I find her confidence appealing.

But to be with a woman like that, you can't keep fucking up. Our first night together wasn't the best, but hopefully she believes I could satisfy her in bed if I had another chance. However, given some of the problems I had in my twenties, I'm not as confident as I wish I could be, though even if I can't perform in certain ways, I can still pleasure her.

Jon elbows me in the side. "The morning after the wedding, I saw you walking with Kim Sung to Tim Hortons. What's happening there? Did you make up for last time?" He waggles his eyebrows in a disturbing way.

I don't deign to reply. I don't even give him the satisfaction of looking annoyed.

I hope everything will go well when I see Kim at the next wedding, but I have the oddest feeling that something will go horribly wrong.

Chapter 14

Kim

FREDDIE IS VISITING FROM B.C., which means that for dim sum, we're going to Freddie's favorite restaurant, and my parents are fussing over him. They order all his favorites, and when I reach for the char siu bao, Mom whisks it away and puts it in front of him.

"It's so nice to have you back," she says, "but you should have brought your girlfriend."

Freddie picks up a har gow with his chopsticks. "She's busy."

"Aiyah! Surely she could have made time to meet your family."

Perhaps because I haven't seen my baby brother in a while, I feel the need to defend him. It's silly of me, though. Freddie is the favorite; he doesn't need my defense.

"It's a long flight," I say. "They're on the other side of the country."

"We'll have to fly out to visit," Mom says, and Dad nods in agreement.

Freddie is here for ten days and will be attending Isobel's wedding next Saturday. He and Isobel are the same age, and I guess he decided that if he was going to attend only one of the weddings this summer, it would be hers. Not that he and Isobel are super close, but I did catch them smoking up together once in high school.

"You need a haircut." Mom reaches over to touch his shaggy hair. "Before the wedding."

"'Kay," he says, not looking up from his food.

My brother is thirty, but sometimes, he still seems like a teenager to me.

"Are you going to marry her?" Mom asks. "I'll give you advice on rings."

Freddie's facial expression finally changes, a tiny notch appearing between his brows. "She doesn't believe in marriage."

"She doesn't believe in marriage?" Mom screeches. "What are you doing to change her mind?"

Freddie shrugs. "Nothing."

"Don't you want to get married and have children?"

Dad pats Mom's shoulder and says something quietly. He's probably telling her to make less of a ruckus in the restaurant, but knowing her, that will just make her louder.

"You don't need to get married to have kids," I point out unhelpfully.

Mom opens her mouth and closes it a bunch of times. When she finally speaks, she turns her attention to me, unfortunately. "You haven't dated anyone for a while."

"No, I haven't."

"Maybe you should get back together with Troy," Dad says.

Mom nods. "Yes, I liked him."

"No, you didn't," I say. "Not particularly."

"But he's the best you can do, and I want at least one of my kids to get married."

"*The best I can do?* I could do a hell of a lot better than Troy—"

"Don't swear, Kim."

"—if I were trying."

"Then try!"

I look down at my teacup. I never told my mother that I swore off relationships; I'm not prepared for the chaos that would result. But could it really get much worse?

"What are the best apps for dating?" Mom asks. "I'll make a profile for you."

"No—"

"Tinder? Is that the best one?"

Freddie laughs into his teacup, and I refrain from telling my mother that I already have a Tinder profile.

"Susan's daughter used a matchmaking service." Mom clucks her tongue. "It was very expensive, but if this is what we need—"

"No," I say.

A lot of conversations with my mother involve me saying "no" and her not listening.

"Relax, Mom," Freddie says. "I'm sure Kim has it under control." He's the only person who can tell my mother to relax without her completely losing it.

Mom shakes her head. "I'll ask my friends if they know any nice single men for you."

"Please, no," I say, but I can't stop Max from popping into my head. If my mom had any idea what happened with him, I'd probably expire on the spot.

She ignores my response, as usual. "Don't worry, I'll ask."

I sigh. I'm tired of fighting. It was nice to have Mom's attention on Freddie for a little while, but now she's back to fretting over me.

The server sets another bamboo steamer on our table, and I focus my attention on that. Maybe if I stare at it hard enough, I can disappear.

Wednesday at work, I get a text from Freddie. He asks if he can come over tonight and sleep on my couch, much to my surprise. We never hang out without Mom and Dad, and we rarely even text each other.

But I don't dislike my brother, and spending a lot of time with our parents would get to anyone, so I agree.

He arrives after dinner, knapsack slung over one shoulder, most of his hair gone.

"So, you got that haircut after all," I say.

"Figured I might as well. Was gonna get a little trim soon anyway."

"That looks like more than a little trim."

He shrugs before pulling out a joint.

"On the balcony. Not in here," I say.

"I know, I know."

I sit outside with him—it's been a long time since both of my balcony chairs have been occupied—and ensure the door is shut behind me. When he holds out the joint, I take it from him.

He seems surprised.

"What?" I say after I inhale.

"You've always been the good one."

I snort. "And you've always been the favorite."

He shrugs again before mumbling something. I don't catch most of it, but I think I hear "patriarchy," which is a bigger word than Freddie usually uses.

Hmm.

We sit in silence for while before he says, "You wanna know something?"

I expect him to tell me without me needing to say "yes," but when it becomes apparent that he's waiting for an answer, I gesture for him to continue.

"I don't have a girlfriend," he says.

I start coughing. I blame the smoke. "What?"

"Yeah, just thought it would make my life easier if I told a little lie."

I can't believe he's actually pretending to be in a relationship. Sure, the possibility occurred to me, but I thought I was being ridiculous.

"What will you do when they visit?" I ask.

"We'll break up before then."

"You little shit," I mutter affectionately.

His lips quirk. "You can do it, too. Invent a boyfriend, girlfriend, whatever. That way no one will threaten to"—he cracks up—"start a Tinder account for you."

"But I live here, and if they hadn't met him for two months, they'd take matters into their own hands. Hire a private investigator. Wait outside my door until they saw him."

"Then find a guy to act the part," he says.

"I wouldn't subject anyone to that."

"You could pay him."

"I'm not made of money."

He shrugs yet again. "You've got a nice place."

"It's tiny. Mom doesn't like the direction I face, either. Can't remember why, but she doesn't."

"Mom needs to chill out."

"Sneak some CBD oil into her congee."

He laughs.

"You know it's not that simple," I say. "If I have a boyfriend, they'll just bother me about different things. Like wedding planning."

"Yeah, I can see that." He pauses. "Are you just not built for romance, like me?"

I nearly say yes, but I get the feeling he means it in a different way than I do.

This isn't what I expected, and I wonder how well I really know my brother. Not that we've ever been close, but still.

"I don't object to the *idea* of romance," I say slowly, "but the reality of it."

Freddie mumbles something else about the patriarchy.

"My relationships always end up pissing the shit out of me," I tell him. "I want a guy who supports me. Who won't expect me to do three-quarters of the housework if we move in together, while expecting to be repeatedly praised for the tiny amount he does."

"I hope you find it."

"I'm not looking for it anymore."

But for some reason, I think of Max.

I turn toward my brother. He hasn't told me exactly how he identifies, but… "I get it, Freddie. I'm glad you told me." I place my hand on top of his.

He smiles at me before passing over the joint. "Thanks."

Freddie takes out his phone and starts watching cat videos, so I take out my phone, too. I find myself going to Instagram and checking if Max has an account.

He does!

I'm somewhat surprised. I thought he'd be one of those people who look down on social media. He doesn't post very much, though. A few pictures around Toronto, some pictures of food. I follow him and send him a message. **Heyyyy.**

He follows me and messages me back not five minutes later.

MAX: Hi

ME: You're on Instagram! Are you on TikTok too? If so, I won't tell. Your secret's safe with me.

MAX: Right

ME: So you ARE on TikTok?

MAX: Of course not.

ME: What are you doing tonight, if you're not making TikTok videos?

MAX: Ironing my underwear like a normal person.

Is that a joke? I'm not entirely sure. I think back to his discarded boxer briefs on the night of Tessa and Malcolm's wedding. Were those ironed? But if he'd been wearing them all day, how would I be able to tell? And while he irons his underwear, is he wearing nothing below the waist, like Winnie-the-Pooh?

I giggle.

MAX: That was a joke, in case you weren't sure.

ME: Next time, please add a winky emoji so I know.

ME: I just did a search, and some people do recommend ironing your underwear. Seems like a hassle. Anyway, what are you actually up to?

MAX: Reading

ME: Don't let me keep you. I'm just dicking around on my phone.

MAX: It's fine. I finished a chapter.

ME: Do you ever stop reading in the middle of a chapter just for funsies?

MAX: Only if the chapters are really long. Then I stop at a scene break.

I picture him sitting on a recliner, wearing dress pants and a button-down shirt. An empty mug and a novel on the table beside him, his brows drawn downward as he looks at his phone.

I find the image appealing, truth be told, mainly because of the contrast with the filthy things he whispered to me at the last wedding. I shouldn't be so intrigued by the idea of sleeping with him again, but I am.

I set down my phone and gaze at the building next to mine. Mmm. This chair feels really nice...

"The wedding's this weekend, right?" Tessa says to me on Thursday. We all work from home on Fridays, so we tend to talk about our weekend plans on Thursdays at the office. The two of us are in the break room for lunch.

"Yeah," I say.

She makes a face. "The forecast doesn't look good."

"It doesn't. Luckily, the wedding is inside." Isobel and Daisy are getting married in a church, and the reception is at a Chinese banquet hall. Still, the torrential downpour won't be pleasant for going in and out of venues, and it'll limit some of the pictures.

"Max will be there?" Tessa asks with an expression of innocence.

"Mm-hmm."

I'm not sure what Max has told Malcolm, and if Malcolm has, in turn, shared that information with his wife. Tessa knows we slept together, and she knows I had the surprise of my life when Max turned up at the last wedding I attended. But I've abstained from telling her some of the details I told Iris, since Max is Malcolm's friend.

I don't dread seeing Max again. In fact, a part of me might even be excited.

Tessa pokes me in the side. "Are you daydreaming about him?"

"Of course not." I hope the forcefulness of my denial isn't suspicious.

"I can't wait to make a speech at your wedding and tell people that I'm the reason you met." She claps her hands. "It's just *perfect*, since you caught the bouquet."

"Don't remind me," I mutter.

I've known Tessa for years. She doesn't usually try to convince people that they'll change their minds about love, but ever since her nuptials, it's like she wants to see romance everywhere.

I'm glad my friend is happy, but it's not for me, even if the thought of glancing across the apartment and seeing Max ironing his underwear is rather endearing.

Hmph. I think my brain has gone rogue.

Chapter 15

Max

I LOOK IN THE mirror. My tie is lopsided, and the color isn't quite working, either. Sighing, I return to my closet and after much deliberation, select a tie in a slightly different shade of blue. Emphasis on *slightly*.

My next attempt at a knot is better, but I'm still not satisfied, so I remove the tie and decide to throw caution to the wind by wearing a purple one.

Yes, that's right. Purple. I don't know what the world has come to.

It takes me three attempts to get the knot right. Then I put on my shoes, grab an umbrella, and ride the elevator down to the garage.

My heart is thumping quickly, and I know it's because of Kim. I'll see her for the first time since Mirabel's wedding.

When I leave my building, it's nearly an hour before the ceremony starts, and it's only a twenty-minute drive. I expect delays due to the heavy rain, and indeed, traffic is a little slow, but I still get to the United church half an hour early.

Not many people are here yet. Gladys and Gilbert, of course, and a few members of the wedding party—including Evan—stand at the front of the church and talk amongst themselves.

There's a loud crack of thunder, and all the chatter stops. The lights go out. Not a brief power flicker—no, once we get to ten seconds, I start to worry, but then the lights come back on. Someone cheers.

"Is that for me?" My dad bows before entering room, arm in arm with my mom.

A giggling Nolan scurries in behind my parents, Auntie Gladys in hot pursuit. My aunt is wearing heels, and she's no match for a three-year-old, who squeezes between my parents and continues to the front of the church. Isobel, who's in a three-piece suit, scoops him up in her arms.

"I'm so sorry," Gladys says. "I know I'm supposed to watch him so you can focus on your wedding day, but he's just so fast."

By five minutes to three, the lights have flickered two more times, but it looks like nearly everyone has made it.

Except Kim.

I pull out my phone—which is already set to silent—and DM her on Instagram because that's the only way I know to reach her.

I'm not surprised when she doesn't reply. She could be driving, but I can't help being concerned for her. I'm pretty sure I saw her parents, as well as a man I think is her brother, but she wasn't with them.

I head to the entrance of the church, open the door...and there she is, climbing up the steps. The only thing that stops me from swearing under my breath is the fact that I'm in a church.

Kim looks absolutely stunning. She's wearing a floral dress with coral flowers and green leaves. On someone else, it might look demure, but on her, it's extremely sexy. She's paired it with strappy heels.

Because I'm too distracted by how incredible she looks, it takes a few seconds before I realize what she's carrying above her head.

A small blue shark umbrella.

There are fins and a tail protruding from the umbrella, plus a set of triangular teeth.

She holds up a hand before I have a chance to speak. "Don't say anything."

Kim's mother hurries over and screams.

"I know you're afraid of sharks," Kim says as she steps into the church and closes the umbrella. "I've heard in extreme detail about the nightmares you got from *Jaws*, but this is just an umbrella."

"But *why*?" Kim's mom asks.

"I couldn't find my black one. My friend's daughter left this at my apartment the other day. Normally I'd just skip the umbrella, but..." She gestures toward the door. "It really is raining."

Her gaze meets mine, and my skin prickles. It's a cool summer's day, but right now, it feels as hot as it did at Mirabel's wedding.

Since I figure Kim will stay with her family, I don't attempt to sit with her, instead returning to the pew where I left my umbrella, next to my parents and Leo.

The organ music begins a few minutes later. Nolan—in black pants, red suspenders, white shirt, and a black bowtie—walks down the aisle with a basket of rose petals. I believe he's supposed to be tossing the petals, but he doesn't, just enjoys the attention. When he gets to the front of the church, he seems to remember the tossing-the-rose-petals part and upends the basket. All the pink petals land in one place on the floor.

"I did it!" he says, and laughter echoes through the church.

Nolan is followed by three bridesmaids, and then Daisy enters in a svelte white dress.

The minister—a woman—begins speaking as Daisy and Isobel stand before her. I try to focus on the ceremony, I really do, but my mind keeps straying to Kim, huddled under the shark umbrella. I imagine her saying "fuck it," tossing the umbrella aside, and letting the rain wash over her, the wet dress clinging to her skin. And I imagine stepping into the rain myself and kissing her...

A few people chuckle, and I'm not sure why because I wasn't paying attention, which isn't like me at all. I should save these thoughts until later.

For the rest of the ceremony, I do—mostly—succeed, and luckily, there are no more power flickers. Isobel and Daisy kiss and the organ music starts again as they exit, the wedding party following behind them.

"Can we eat the cake now?" Nolan asks loudly.

When I arrive at the reception, it's still dark and gloomy, but it's no longer raining. I leave my umbrella in the car, as it would be a pain to carry it around during cocktail hour and I'm not sure there will be a place to check it.

Daisy, Isobel, Gladys, Gilbert, and Nolan greet me.

"Aiyah! Did you see the weather?" Gladys acts like the storm was a personal affront.

"Did you see me throw the pedals?" Nolan asks.

As I place my envelope in the box, my aunt gives me a strange look.

Huh. I have no idea what that's about.

I enter the room where everyone has gathered. I will abstain from cocktails, just have a few sips of champagne, and I will also abstain from canapés, seeing as there will be more than enough to eat later. I plan to be sensible tonight, unlike last time.

"Hey!" Jon comes over with a disturbing smile on his face.

"Hi," I say warily. "What did you do?"

"Why do you think I did anything?" He slaps me on the back. "Let's check out the seating arrangements, shall we?"

I have a bad feeling about this.

We go over to the board, and I scan it for my name. I'm at a table with Leo, my parents, and...

"Shit," I mutter.

Chapter 16

Kim

IT'S A GOOD THING I'm alone when I see the seating chart. Well, there are lots of other people in the room, but nobody's paying attention to me, and it's loud enough that I don't think anyone hears the curse words that escape my mouth.

When I arrive at the table in the dining room a few minutes later, my parents and Max's parents are already there. Yep, it's a meet-the-parents situation with my one-night stand. Also present are Freddie and one of Max's brothers.

This is basically my definition of hell.

"I'm Howie." Max's father is introducing himself to my parents. "I believe we met once, many years ago?"

"Good, good, you're all here!" Gladys appears out of nowhere and claps her hands. "At Mirabel's wedding, I saw Kim and Max talking *very* closely outside..."

Max steps up to the table right as she says that.

"...and I thought I'd sit you all at the same table today so you can get to know each other." She seems far too pleased with herself, smiling as she walks away.

My mom also seems pleased as she looks Max up and down.

"You're Gladys's oldest nephew?" she says. "The engineer?"

"Yes," he replies.

He's everything she wants in a son-in-law. I will never hear the end of it. And we'll all be trapped at a table together for the next three hours or so, seeing as this is a ten-course Chinese wedding banquet.

I wish the shark umbrella in my purse would come to life and eat me.

I move to take my seat, but when I pull out the chair, Max clears his throat and says, "I believe you're over here."

I frown. I could have sworn…

Oh. His face betrays nothing, but I'm pretty sure he switched our name cards when no one else was looking. I'm now next to his brother rather than his mother.

An odd warmth fills my chest, and I give him a swift nod in thanks.

Max doesn't look much like his dad, a jolly man in his sixties with receding gray hair. I can't imagine Max would ever be *jolly*. His mother, who's wearing a navy dress, appears to be the more serious of the two. I wonder how I can win—

Wait a second. Why do I care about winning them over?

I turn to my left, and my gaze locks with Max's. Damn, he does look good in that suit. It's the same one he wore to Tessa and Malcolm's wedding. I have no doubt that he, too, isn't happy with this situation, and perhaps he's a little anxious, but his expression says, *We're in this together.*

I decide to clear up the confusion so nobody gets false hopes. Keeping close to the truth is probably the safest option.

"Look," I say, "Auntie Gladys just caught us talking outside the tent last time. We met at a wedding in June—his friend married my friend—and we were saying hello to each other again. There's nothing more to it than that."

"Is that so?" Howie's eyes are twinkling.

Before I can say anything else, Max answers, "Yes. That's correct."

"But my sister said you two were talking very closely…"

"Because the music was loud," Max says. "It was the only way to be heard."

"Outside the tent? Lynne and I stepped out for a few minutes, and it wasn't that bad."

"Well." Max clears his throat. "I think they turned the volume down later. It was very loud when the dancing started."

I stifle a laugh. He says everything seriously, but he's not the greatest liar.

"Kim is an engineer, too," Mom jumps in. "A structural engineer."

"Ah, like Max," Howie says. "No wonder they hit it off."

"We didn't hit it off," I mumble, but no one is paying attention to me, the topic of conversation.

"She was always a very good student in school," Mom says.

This is true—aside from that one mark in English—but it's strange to hear my mother sing my praises. I'm not used to it. I look across the table at Freddie, who's being ignored for once. He seems perfectly content with this turn of events.

I can't believe I'm spending the next few hours with these people. I could have refused to sit at the same table as my former one-night stand and his parents and brother, but making a big fuss about seating arrangements doesn't seem like the right thing to do at Isobel and Daisy's wedding. The focus should be on them, not on Isobel's mom's matchmaking efforts.

I'll just have to bear this. Somehow. For the first time ever, I find myself hoping that the emcee talks a *lot*.

A server comes around with wine. After he pours me a glass, I immediately take a sip. My mom shoots me a glare that says, *Make a good impression. Why are you so eager to drink?*

Whatever.

"Kim is also a very good pianist," Dad says.

I nearly choke on my wine.

"Yes." Mom beams. "She did grade eight piano."

They're overstating my accomplishments. True, I passed grade eight piano, but barely. I have zero natural talent, and now that I haven't touched a piano in over a decade, I doubt I could play much beyond "Mary Had a Little Lamb" or "Jingle Bells." Perhaps I could manage a few bars of "The Imperial March."

"So if their children take piano lessons," Mom says, "she can help them practice."

This time, I actually do choke on my wine.

"It seems they have a lot in common," Howie says. "Max is very good at piano, too."

That doesn't surprise me. I'm sure he's better than I am.

"Their children will be musical prodigies." Dad laughs.

For fuck's sake. Why are they talking about our hypothetical offspring?

But luck is on my side for once: the emcee walks up to the microphone, which puts an end to this horrifying conversation.

"Hello, everyone," he says. "I'm Lloyd, a long-time friend of Isobel's, and I'll be your emcee for the evening. If everyone could please take your seats, the food will be out in just a few minutes."

There's silence at our table for about 0.2 seconds before my mother says, "Speaking of food, Kim is also a very good cook."

Good thing I wasn't imbibing any wine when she said that.

"I wouldn't go that far," I murmur, rather than calling her a liar. I have some extremely basic competency in the kitchen—I can scramble eggs and cook rice (in a rice cooker) without embarrassing myself—but that's about it. It's never been of interest to me, much to my mother's disappointment.

"She's just modest," Mom says to Max's parents.

Ha!

"Max is also accomplished in the kitchen," Howie says.

Yep, Max Mok is good at everything.

Except sex.

That's unfair of me, even if our night together was underwhelming. I'm sure he'll do better next time.

Wait, why am I thinking about *next time*?

I can't deny that I feel some heat coming from the man sitting on my left, but I blame that on anxiety, not attraction. Sure, I've spent a lot of time remembering the words he whispered to me last time. *I'd utterly wreck you.* But I only thought of it twice yesterday—I'm improving.

"It's good when a man can give his wife a break from cooking occasionally," Mom says. The idea of a man actually doing the bulk of the cooking isn't a consideration to her.

A server walks over to our table with a platter filled with cold meats and jellyfish. Swiftly, he puts an equal amount of food on each of the eight small plates, leaving a little on the platter. I usually like this stuff, but my appetite is poor right now. I push the food around with my chopsticks.

"You okay?" Max murmurs.

I'm touched that he's asking, but if we whisper to each other, our parents will probably take it as a sign we're married getting next summer, something I wish to avoid.

As soon as the dishes from the first course are cleared, my mother stands up.

"Kim, could you show me where the washroom is?"

I don't know where it is, but I suspect she just wants to talk to me alone. Since I don't wish to cause a fuss, I stand up.

As it turns out, my mom knows the location of the women's washroom, and as soon as we're inside, she says, "What are you doing?"

"Nothing. I'm not doing anything."

"That's the problem! Show that you'll make a nice wife and daughter-in-law. Don't you want to get married?"

I don't answer that question.

"You're getting old!" Mom cries. "Do you want to end up alone with no children to look after you? You haven't brought a man home in years, and Max comes from a good family and has a good job. It was so nice of Gladys to sit us all together. She knows I worry about you."

"You don't need to. I'm fine."

Mom pats my shoulder. She isn't usually affectionate, so this catches me off guard. "Stay here to compose yourself and fix your hair—"

"What's wrong with my hair?"

"—and come back to the table soon."

When she exits the room, I take a look in the mirror. My hair is a bit frizzy, and I do my best to get it under control before leaving the washroom.

I nearly trip over Max in the hallway.

"Hey." He reaches out to steady me. "Your mom said I should check on you."

"You didn't have to listen to her."

"Are you okay? I had no knowledge of my aunt's plans, I promise."

I never thought he did. "I'm fine."

"If you make excuses and leave the wedding, I won't be in-sulted."

"I can handle it."

"I just..." He runs a hand through his hair. "I noticed you didn't eat anything."

"There are lots of courses. I'll get enough food, don't you worry."

He frowns. "What can I do to make it better?"

I stare at him.

"What?" he asks.

What can I do to make it better? His tone might not be full of warmth, but that's just Max. I appreciate his concern. I'm not used to my boyfriends asking such questions. Not that Max Mok is my boyfriend, of course.

But the guys I dated in the past...whenever I was with their families, I felt like it was them against me. My so-called partner wouldn't be on my side.

"I don't think there's anything you can do." I pause. "But I have a question for you. Your mom is very quiet. Is that a sign she doesn't like me?"

I don't know why I care. I *don't* care. I'm just curious.

He shakes his head. "She's not very outgoing. Large events aren't her favorite."

Okay. That's good to know. "The way my parents are talking about children and weddings...it's making my skin crawl. It's probably doing the same to you."

I swear he hesitates before nodding. "It does." He crosses his arms over his chest, and I should not be admiring the way his jacket is stretching across his shoulders, but I am. "Are you ready to go back? Or do you need another minute?"

"I'm fine," I say, "but I don't want us walking in together. You go first, and I'll be there soon."

"Very well." He dips his head and strides back into the reception.

I stare after him, my gaze lingering even once he's disappeared from view. There's a strange flutter in my stomach. I haven't eaten anything since before the ceremony, but I know this isn't due to hunger.

Max cares about what *I* want. That shouldn't be so remarkable, but when you're used to your family and romantic partners not giving a shit...well, it matters.

It's enough to warm my cynical heart.

By the time we've finished three more courses, my mother is prattling on about how I enjoy *hiking,* of all things.

In truth, I don't understand the appeal. I much prefer the elliptical machine. The last time I went on a hike, I got eaten alive by mosquitos. (Yes, I wore insect repellent. It didn't help.)

But rather than interrupting to set the record straight, I stay quiet. I'm not sure what my mother's trying to prove. That I'm in good shape? That I'm well-rounded and have many diverse interests? It's rather fascinating to hear her talk about me like this.

I mean, fascinating and horrifying at the same time.

"Do you actually like hiking?" Max murmurs, leaning close to me.

"No," I say.

His soft laughter makes my breath catch.

We're saved from further conversation when the emcee announces some games for the happy couple, but those finish by the time the lobster is served.

"Do you know if Isobel and Daisy plan to have more children?" Mom asks.

Nobody has any idea.

"How many children do you want, Max?" Mom presses.

"I... Mmm. This lobster is *really* good," Max says. "Isn't it, Kim?"

He's probably uncomfortable with the question, too, but I have the sense he's doing this mostly for me, and I suppress a smile.

Some people can make a conversation flow in the way they like, as though it's effortless, but not Max. Although it's stilted, I appreciate that he's trying.

"Yes, the lobster is excellent." I struggle for a topic. Lobster ...P.E.I. "Have you ever been to the Maritimes?" I talk about our family trip there—fifteen years ago—for a while, only stopping when I think my mother might have finally forgotten her question about children.

Alas, as soon as there's a pause in the conversation, she jumps in.

"How many kids do you want?" she asks Max.

Sensing that he won't be able to get out of this, I suppose, he answers, "Two, I think."

When I turn in his direction, I notice he's sweating, and yes, it's warm in the crowded banquet hall, but I don't think that's the reason. I suspect this situation freaks him out more than he's trying to let on, and something clenches in my chest.

"Are *you* okay?" I ask him quietly.

"Yes. Don't worry about me."

Those clipped words don't help me worry less.

"Dinner won't last forever," I say. "Just another hour or two. It'll pass like this." I snap my fingers.

I chuckle awkwardly at my terrible attempt at humor, but he shoots me a smile that might make my knees weak if I weren't already sitting. He's so handsome, in a rather nerdy and starchy way. It's really working for me tonight.

Once again, I feel like we're in this together.

After soup for dessert, the banquet is finally over, and I nearly weep with relief. There's also wedding cake, which is being sliced up in the kitchen right now, but it'll be served after the dancing starts. We all stand up, and some of the tables are moved to the side.

My mother approaches Max. "Kim came here by transit. Perhaps you could give her a ride home later?"

"You don't have to," I say quickly. "I can catch an Uber. I probably don't live anywhere close to you."

"I'll drive you," he says, then promptly walks away.

I feel bereft at his absence, after sitting next to him for so long, and the feeling catches me by surprise, as does my anticipation of being alone in a car with him.

The lights are turned down as Isobel steps onto the dance floor with Daisy, who changed into a red cheongsam for the reception. I don't recognize the song, but as they begin dancing—something which they have clearly been practicing—I'm strangely moved. I'm not usually affected by such things, but they look so happy to be here together, celebrating their love with friends and family. Watching them move across the dance floor, looking into each other's eyes...it's a beautiful sight.

Daisy stumbles, but Isobel is quick to catch her. They share a quiet laugh, and I don't know them well, but I believe in their relationship. I believe they will always be there to support each other; I believe in the vows they made earlier today. When Isobel murmurs something in Daisy's ear, Daisy tips her head back and smiles, looking even more luminous than before.

A tear threatens to fall from my eye, and I discreetly wipe it away.

For the first time in years, I wish I had a special moment like this with my own partner. And to my dismay, the man in my imagination looks like Max.

Chapter 17

Max

I NEED AIR.

I hurry out of the banquet hall and lean against the building. I can't believe that just happened.

When I saw the seating arrangements, I was, of course, not happy. Sitting at a table with my parents, the woman I have a bit of a crush on, as well as her parents...it isn't my idea of fun. I was also acutely aware that it wasn't *her* idea of fun, so I tried to make sure it went as well for Kim as I could. I tried to show her that I was on her side, that we were a team, and...

Oh, I don't fucking know. After trying to keep it together for the last few hours, I'm a mess. Sweat is dripping down the back of my neck, and I almost feel like vomiting, though perhaps that's due to the sheer quantity of food I consumed more than anything else.

Evan comes outside and stands next to me. "You okay?"

That's the question of the evening, the question that Kim and I kept asking each other. Even when we weren't speaking, it felt like we were asking it with our looks.

She's so gorgeous tonight. At one point, I nearly touched the inside of her knee without realizing what I was doing, but I pulled myself back just in time.

"I will be," I say.

Jon comes out the door. "That looked rough."

Yeah, it must have, if even Jon isn't attempting to tease me.

Leo joins us, too. He leans back against the wall beside me and shoves his hands in his pockets. Whenever he wears a suit, he looks uncomfortable, and tonight is no exception. Now that dinner's done, he's loosened his tie. I suspect that Kim's parents would not have been as happy with him as a potential partner for their daughter. The man with tattoos and no degree—yeah, that's not what they want, even if he's a good guy.

I wish Evan had been at the table instead of Leo. He would have been more help when it came to the conversation, not that I blame Leo for more or less staying silent.

"So, what's happening between you and Kim?" Jon pulls off his jacket and slings it over his shoulder. "I wasn't going to say anything—"

Leo snickers.

"—but after that dinner, I have to ask. Once again, if you need any pointers, feel free to let me know."

"I'm not that desperate, thank you."

Jon laughs.

Evan pats me on the shoulder. "So, *do* you want to see her again? Without your families present?"

"I do," I say, "but she's not really the dating type."

"That's perfect," Jon says. "You can have a little fun—hopefully more fun than last time—and she doesn't expect any commitment..."

I glare at him.

"Right, right. You're an old man. You want commitment."

Why is he so annoying?

"I'm supposed to drive her home tonight," I say. "I'll ask her out. See what she says."

Everything with Kim has been backward. It started with us sleeping together, and we haven't even gone on a single real date and our parents have already met. I prefer when things proceed the way they're supposed to. I prefer when I can mentally prepare for things like a three-hour dinner with a woman's parents.

We head back inside, and I grab a slice of strawberry champagne cake. Not that I need any more food, but I've always had a bit of a sweet tooth.

Nolan rushes over to me. "Max! I'm having a sleepover with Po Po tonight!"

At least, I think that's what he's saying, but he's a lot shorter than me, and it's hard to tell with the music.

He eyes the cake in my hand. "Can you get me a piece of pink cake, please?"

Daisy appears at my side. "Nolan, you've already had cake."

"Only the chocolate one. I want the pink cake. Pink is my favorite flavor. No—blue is my favorite. But there's no blue cake."

It pains me to hear blue referred to as a "flavor."

"There's some extra cake for us to take home," Daisy says, "but since it's a special day, you can have a bite now, okay?" She picks up a plate with a slice of pink cake, bends down, and holds a small forkful to his lips.

Nolan makes a face. "Why is it so yucky? I thought I liked pink!"

My lips twitch. I finish my cake as Daisy wipes Nolan's mouth, then I search for Kim.

Before I can find her, Aaron approaches me. "Hey, you wanna do a shot?"

"No," I say curtly. I never intend to repeat that drunken experience.

"Is something wrong?" Aaron sounds concerned.

"No." I try to make my voice gentler, despite my agitation. Somehow, it seems paramount that I find Kim as quickly as possible.

"Cake was great, wasn't it?"

I nod, and out of the corner of my eye, I catch a glimpse of Kim.

As soon as I see her, I can't look away. She has a face that makes me wish I were an artist. She's taken her hair down, and I itch to run my fingers through it. I walk over to her, trying to look calm and collected despite my rapid pulse.

"Would you like to dance?" I ask.

In response, she loops her hands around my neck, and I smile. I recall our dance at Malcolm and Tessa's wedding—that time, she asked me. It was only last month, but a lot has happened since, and dancing with her feels different now.

We don't say anything for a long time. It's nice to just hold her. She moves back and forth, the skirt of her pretty dress swishing about her legs. We've spent so much time in close proximity tonight, but I didn't get to touch her until now, and it feels good. It feels right.

It feels like a gift.

She's breathtaking, and she's dancing with *me*, this woman who's consumed my thoughts in the past several weeks. I don't think I could ever tire of dancing with her.

I pull her a little closer. I try not to imagine touching her skin, rather than the thin fabric of her dress, but I can't help it. She smells vaguely of coconut, and I want the scent of her on my pillows one day. I think it's her shampoo; even in those heels, she's quite a bit shorter than me, and the top of her hair is a couple of inches below my nose.

She tilts her head up to meet my gaze, her face so close to mine. It throws off our rhythm, and I can barely even hear the music now.

She's everything.

When she stumbles, it breaks the spell, but I react quickly and wrap an arm securely around her.

"Sorry," she says. "I'm tired."

"Would you like me to drive you home now?"

"If you want to stay—"

"No, no, I'm happy to leave." *If it's with you.*

"Is it past your bedtime, Max?" she teases, walking her fingers up my chest.

"It is."

I keep a straight face, but I'm glad to hear her being a little sassy again. She's more relaxed than she was earlier.

We congratulate the brides and say goodbye to our families. When we exit the banquet hall, it's pouring. It was barely sprinkling when I was out here with my brothers, but now it's a downpour.

"You stay here," I say, "and I'll bring the car to the entrance."

"Where's your umbrella?" Kim asks.

"I left it in the car."

"Good call."

I level her with a glare. "It wasn't raining when I arrived, and it's awkward to carry an umbrella around all night. It's a good quality one. I don't want to lose it." Not one of those cheap, flimsy umbrellas you get at the drugstore; no, when I can afford it, I do my research and get the best I can, even when it comes to umbrellas.

"You can use this one." She pulls the shark umbrella out of her purse and hands it to me, her lips quirking in amusement.

Given its small size, I'm not sure how effective it'll be at keeping me dry, but it's my only option. I don't want to wait until the rain lets up—who knows when that'll be.

I hurry across the lot with the shark perched above me, trying not to step in any puddles out of concern for my shoes. I still get rather wet, but I think I manage as well as I can, given the circumstances. I back out of my parking spot and pull up to the entrance, where Kim is waiting. Thanks to the overhang, she stays mostly dry as she enters the car.

"Now tell me where I'm going," I say.

She directs me to where she lives in the east end. Nowhere near my apartment, but that's okay.

We're quiet in the car; I feel as if talking would mess up my concentration. Focusing on the road is all I can manage after such a long day when I have Kim next to me.

"Apparently there's some flooding downtown," she says.

"Mmm."

That's about the extent of our conversation until I pull up in front of her building and put the car in park. As I turn toward her, my skin prickles. I'm perturbed by how off balance she makes me, but at the same time, I crave more.

I'm also very aware of how this whole thing has not gone the way I'd like...and how I gave her a peek into my dirty fantasies last time. My cheeks heat, but I press forward.

I have to do this. I have to try.

"Would you..." I swallow. "Would you allow me to take you on a date?"

She starts laughing. "Your reaction to all of tonight—and what happened at Tessa and Malcolm's wedding—is to ask me on a *date*?"

"Yes."

She tilts her head. "Are you giving in to family pressure?"

"No. It has nothing to do with that."

"You don't sound as if you like me. You sound as if the words are being dragged from your lips against your will."

I sigh and rake a hand through my hair. This is veering off course.

"Do you like me despite your good sense?" she asks. "Like Darcy?"

I know she's talking about *Pride and Prejudice*—I'm well read—but I don't fancy myself a Jane Austen hero.

"I assure you, that's not the case," I say. "Quite the opposite, in fact." I think she's wonderful, and I don't understand why every single person didn't ask her to dance. "I'm just frustrated with the situation. The fact that I made a bad impression the first time we were together, the fact that our families are involved."

"A bad impression," she teases.

"But I promise, I can do better." I lean forward; I can feel the words I said to her last time in the small space between us. *I would devote myself to your pleasure. I'd have you squirming on my fingers. Writhing against my face...* "What do you think?"

Chapter 18

Kim

I haven't dated since I was twenty-seven.

I have my reasons, and looking at the sharp lines of Max's face in the shadows? That doesn't make me forget those reasons; it would be hard to forget them after tonight.

"If you have to think about it," he says, "that's fine. I'll give you my number, and you can text me your answer. I won't bother you again until you contact me."

"No Instagram DMs?"

"No."

"But why me?"

I'm not fishing for a compliment; I'm genuinely a little confused.

"What do you mean, why you?" he asks.

"For starters, I've slept around a lot."

"And?"

"Some men don't like women who've slept around. Especially guys who..." I don't know how to say it, so I gesture vaguely in his direction. I imagine him marrying a woman who'd be the perfect little daughter-in-law, not...me.

He leans even closer. "I'm not those men, Kimberly."

His voice has an arousing edge to it, and I squeeze my thighs together. I've never cared for my full name...until now. When those three syllables fall from his lips, it feels like he's caressing my skin.

"You know what you like," he says. "I appreciate that you're...boldly sexual, for lack of a better term."

It's not surprising he'd enjoy that for a night; it's just surprising he'd want someone like me as a girlfriend, but that seems to be the case.

"Though to be clear," he continues, "I have no interest in a non-monogamous relationship. I'm not assuming anything about what you may or may not desire, or your ability to be faithful. I just want you to know where I stand."

"Would a single date constitute a relationship to you?"

"No, but for future reference."

I tilt my head to view him at a slightly different angle, as if that will help me understand him. "Given our history, it would be easier to ask out someone else."

"It would."

In the silence that follows, I search his face for traces of doubt, but I don't find any. He's sure about what he wants.

"Are you at all concerned," I say, "about your ability to satisfy me in bed?"

"A little, but like I said, our night together didn't really play to my strengths, and I'm quite good at taking instruction."

I find myself smiling, but his expression is still serious. He cups my cheek and strokes his thumb over my skin. I lean into his touch.

I'm not used to this sort of gentleness, and it's nice. He hasn't done anything *big* tonight, but he's been quietly attentive. For the first time in five years, I believe there's a chance that a new relationship—with Max—could be different from my past experiences.

"Do you think you could do a good job if I invite you up tonight?" I ask.

"No. I'm bloated and tired."

I bark out a laugh. That was honesty I definitely didn't anticipate. I admit to being a touch disappointed, but I try to shove that feeling aside.

Max smiles faintly at my amusement. "You think about it. Text me this week. I'll give you my number—"

"I'll go out with you," I say. "Next Saturday, if that works?"

"It does." His smile broadens, and I can't help feeling pleased that I was the cause of it.

"But I have one condition. Our parents *cannot* know about this. Not until we're beyond a few dates, okay? If they ask, just say you're not sure what's happening. I want to do this without family pressure."

He nods. "That's fair."

I take out my phone, and he dictates his number.

"Don't forget this." He hands me the shark umbrella.

I stow it in my purse, then lean forward to kiss him on the lips. It's different from our first kiss, by that small lake up north, the kiss that made me excited for our single night together. I know him better now, and there's a deeper sort of desire in this kiss, in the way his mouth coaxes a moan out of me. It feels like something has shifted between us. He tastes of strawberries and, somehow, of possibilities.

When he pulls back and brushes a lock of hair back from my face, it takes me a moment to remember where I am.

"Good night," he says. "See you soon."

I feel a little giddy as I exit the vehicle. I wave at him once I'm inside the lobby, and he lifts a hand before driving away.

I'm still smiling when I reach my apartment.

ME: Is Saturday still good for you?

MAX: Yes. Would you like to come over for dinner? I can cook us something. Or I can take you out?

He sent that message last night. I should reply, but I still haven't decided what I'd prefer. I read his text over and over as I bite into my sandwich.

"Hey." Iris joins me in the break room. "What's up?"

"For a first date, do you think I should go to his place and let him cook for me, or go out to a restaurant?"

"You're going on a date?" she asks incredulously.

"Sure, why not?"

"Because you never do this. You haven't been on a date in the entire time I've known you. Who is it?"

"Just some guy I met at the wedding on Saturday."

I don't tell her it's Max. It feels awkward to admit that. If, by some miracle, this works out, I'll tell her, but not yet.

"Go to the restaurant," she says. "Meet him there, rather than having him pick you up. Safety first."

"I trust him. I know him...better than you think."

"I thought you just met him?"

"That wasn't the first time."

She gives me a quizzical look, but I ignore it and stare at my phone. I'm leaning toward going to Max's apartment. I'm curious to see it, and it'll also be convenient for sex. Plus, there's something irresistible about a guy cooking for me—it's been a long time since that happened.

ME: Your place

MAX: Anything you don't eat so I can plan the menu?

ME: Olives. Grapefruit. Brussels sprouts.

MAX: Noted.

ME: I'll bring dessert.

ME: In case you were wondering, that wasn't a euphemism.

MAX: I didn't assume it was.

I imagine him saying that with a very straight face and suppress a laugh.

Iris looks up from her bowl. "You have to tell me more about this guy."

"One day," I say. "Maybe. I hope."

Monday evening, I'm wondering what I should eat for dinner and how many more days I can put off grocery shopping when my phone rings. I'm not surprised to see it's my mother.

"Hi." I plop down on my couch.

"Kim! How did it go on Saturday night?" she asks.

"At the wedding? You were there the whole time. No need to ask."

"Aiyah! You know what I mean."

Of course I do. I just can't resist being smart with my mother on occasion. I should resist such temptations, but I don't.

"I got home safely," I say.

My mom sighs in frustration. "Did you invite him in?"

"For coffee? For a nightcap?"

"What's a nightcap?"

"Look, he dropped me off, that's all."

Did my mother *want* me to invite him in and sleep with him? Is she that keen to have Max as a son-in-law? Or is she worried that if I sleep with him too early, he won't think I'm marriage material?

I figure it's best I don't know, so I change the topic. "Did Freddie get to the airport okay?"

"Traffic was bad, but we got him there." Mom sniffs. "I can't believe he lives so far away. He said his girlfriend is from Waterloo, so maybe they'll move back here one day?"

"Right." I'm sure that'll happen. Freddie and his nonexistent girlfriend.

"He won't let us talk to her on the phone," Mom says, "but maybe she can talk to you, and you can report back."

"Uh, okay. I'll ask."

"Are you seeing Max again?" she inquires, smoothly moving the conversation back to my romantic life.

"I don't know." My goal is to provide as little information as possible for now.

"Did you at least get his number?" She sounds exasperated. "Or give him yours?"

"I have his number." If I said no, she might ask Gladys to procure his number for me, and I don't want to make this any more complicated than it needs to be.

"Have you called or texted him yet?"

"Mom, stop it. I can handle it."

"Do you not like him? What's wrong? Is he too serious for you? I—"

"Max is fine. When there's something to report, I'll tell you."

"Alright." My mother sounds doubtful, but this seems to placate her...for now.

We chat for a little longer, and by the time I get off the phone, I'm not in the mood for any kind of cooking, not even frying a couple of eggs. Takeout it is.

I wonder what Max will cook for me on Saturday night, though to be honest, the food isn't the main thing on my mind.

Chapter 19

Max

SINCE MY FIRST SEXUAL encounter with Kim was a bit underwhelming, I'm afraid I'll get in my head and have problems again today. This, of course, is the last thing I want.

So, I make sure I have a relatively low-stress day and try not to obsess over anything. I go to the gym for a quick workout, then head to the grocery store, where I get everything I need for tonight. Back at home, I have lunch, followed by laundry, cleaning, and a little reading. Typical weekend activities.

Just after six o'clock, I start preparing the food. I warned Kim not to come too early because I'm not very good at entertaining someone while I'm cooking.

She arrives at seven, wearing a blue sundress with thin straps. It ends just below her knees, and the instant I see her, I think about how convenient it would be to kneel down and get her off. Or bend her over the counter.

Instead, I nod at the box in her hand, the one that says "Happy As Pie."

"I'll take that," I say. Our fingers brush as she hands it over.

"Strawberry rhubarb," she says.

That's actually my favorite, but it feels weird to say that now, so I don't mention it. She pulls a pint of vanilla ice cream out of her bag, and I put it in the freezer for later. Then I pour her a glass of wine before turning on the wok. Yesterday, I debated what to cook, ultimately deciding that my eggplant and minced pork recipe was the way to go. It's not *my* recipe, exactly, just a modification of something I found online, but I do it well.

She sits at the kitchen island. It's a bit unnerving to have her here as I work, and she seems to pick up on my anxiety.

"I really don't know shit about cooking," she says. "As long as you don't start a fire, I won't notice that anything's amiss."

I sense that she's a bit nervous, too. Her first proper date in years. She's hiding it, behind smiles and a dress with a particularly low neckline—I approve, of course—but I can tell.

She sips her wine. "Do you work from home?"

"Yes. I didn't before the pandemic, but I do now. Aside from the occasional site visit and meetings that can't be done over Teams."

"You like it that way?"

"I do."

"It wasn't for me. I mean, it was good in the short term, and I do like working at home every Friday now, but I get twitchy if I spend too much time in the apartment. It's nice wearing whatever you like to work, though, isn't it?" When I don't immediately answer, she says, "Are you one of those people who wouldn't dare work in his pajamas?"

"I dress like I'm going to the office, even if I no longer have an office to go to."

"Like, nice pants and a collared shirt? Do you put on *shoes*?"

"I don't go that far."

"Sensible."

She gets up and examines my Blu-ray collection. It isn't huge, but I don't trust things not to disappear on streaming services, so I've bought what I want to watch again. I try not to get distracted by the pretty woman wandering around my apartment, the sleek line of her back, the way she sips her wine. Those enticing buttons on the back of her dress? I'm definitely reining in my thoughts about those.

I remove the eggplant from the wok and tip in the ground pork, then switch to the pan with the gai lan. "Just a few more minutes."

When I'm finished, I set the serving dishes on the table, followed by chopsticks and a bowl of rice for each of us.

"Do you want tea with dinner?" I ask.

"Wine is good for me." She smiles as she takes a seat. "This looks great. Thank you."

It feels nice to cook for her. I would have been happy to meet at a restaurant if that's what she preferred, but I like being home, in my own territory. Just the two of us, no one else to interact with—unlike last Saturday.

I nearly shudder at the memory.

We talk about our families a little, then our jobs. It's more activity than my apartment has seen in a while, and Kim's laughter seems to fill up the space.

"I'm going to heat up the pie," I say as I clear the dishes.

"You heat up strawberry-rhubarb pie? I've never done that."

"It's better this way. I don't have to heat up your half, though." It's a small pie—just the right size for two people to split.

"No, go ahead. I'll try it."

As it turns out, Kim agrees that it's better warm, and it's a treat to see her eat dessert. She closes her eyes and moans; I shift uncomfortably in my seat. I hadn't realized that watching a woman eat pie à la mode could be an erotic experience, but it is. I have to remind myself to eat rather than watch her.

After we finish, she tries to help me clean up.

"No, you're a guest," I say, "and I don't like anyone else in my kitchen."

"Are you very particular about how things are done?" she teases.

"Perhaps."

Some people, upon learning that I can be a bit particular, insist on creating further chaos in my space to get on my nerves, but although Kim has definitely brought some chaos to my life, she's not pushing it too far, and I appreciate that.

I pour us each a little more wine, and we retire to the couch. Without any food between us, it feels a bit awkward.

Because, you know, *sex*.

That's the big thing looming between us. I'm not entirely sure if she wants to tackle that today, though. I'm not tired—unlike after the wedding—and I'd be more than happy to partake in such activities, but how to bring it up?

"Would you like to watch a movie?" I ask instead.

"Max." She turns to face me. "Do you actually want to watch a movie? You sound rather cross about it."

"I'm happy to watch a movie with you."

"That's not why I wanted to come to your place rather than a restaurant." She sets down her wine glass and slide closer to me. "I have something else I'd rather do."

My entire body heats up at those words.

She climbs onto my lap, wraps her arms around me, and kisses me slowly, her lips parting against mine before coming back together.

I try to exist just in this moment, just in this kiss. Her tongue swirls around mine, and that moan—I think it's mine, not hers, but I'm not sure. I slide my hands up the back of her thighs, then give her ass a slow, filthy squeeze. When she responds by squirming against my erection, I hiss out a breath.

I've thought about being with her again, of course, but none of those imaginings—while I was in the shower, hand on my cock—compare to the reality of actually having her here.

"Let's move to the bedroom." I stand up, lifting her with me.

I stride down the hallway and deposit her on the bed. I remove my glasses, ready to get down to business. Then I'm on top of her, all over her, and she giggles before moaning. I tug down the straps of her dress and remove her bra, without any difficulties this time. Remembering what she told me by the lavender fields, I set my mouth to her right nipple, and she gasps.

"Good?" I look up. I want to make sure this is amazing for her.

"Mmm." She pushes my head back down.

I lick around the tight bud of her nipple before moving to the other one and sucking it into my mouth. I brush the wet peak with my finger, loving how responsive she is. Her sounds, the way she moves against me. Unlike the first time, I feel like I'm in tune with her.

I return to her lips, kissing her mouth as I hold her wrists above her head. She's so hot and eager, and I'm overwhelmed—in a good way—by the sensations she's causing within me. I roll my hips against her, pressing her down onto the bed, before I sit up and tug her to the edge of the mattress. I kneel on the floor before her and flip up the skirt of her dress. I need to get my mouth on her, and fuck, I can see the wet spot in her panties.

"These have to go," I say.

"Yes," she breathes. "They definitely do."

I remove her underwear and toss them aside. She's still wearing her dress, bunched up around her waist, but her tits and pussy are on display. She looks incredible, flushed with desire and spread out on my bed. I run my middle finger along her entrance before easing it inside; she groans. I stroke in and out of her at a leisurely pace, then pick up the speed.

She touches my wrist. "Let me show you."

I remove my hand and lick my finger. She likes that; I can tell from the way her breath hitches. In fact, I'm so distracted by it that it takes a moment before I can focus on her hand between her legs. Even then, I'm so turned on by Kim touching herself that I have to remind myself to pay attention to her technique.

It's okay that she has to show you, I tell myself. *Don't let it bother you.*

People like different things, and I will dedicate myself to learning what she prefers.

The sight of Kim touching herself really is mesmerizing. Her pink fingernail, sliding inside her body; the sheen coating her finger. She's not at all embarrassed. No, she's comfortable finger-fucking herself in front of me.

"Do you touch yourself a lot?" I ask.

"Yeah. I have a high sex drive. It takes a lot to keep me satisfied."

"You have toys?" I'm positive of the answer, but I ask anyway.

"I do. I brought one with me to the hotel in Milton, and after our conversation outside... I don't usually fuck myself so hard, but I could still feel it when we had breakfast together."

I release a growl as I think of her alone in the hotel room. Getting herself off—because of *me*—then sitting across from me the next morning without saying a damn word.

This woman is too much.

My cock aches, but I refuse to touch myself yet. Instead, I remove her hand from her pussy. "My turn." I curl my finger inside her channel, just the way she likes it, and stroke her clit with my thumb. "Is that good?"

"Yeah, just like...that." She squeezes her eyes shut, her sooty eyelashes fluttering against her cheeks as she grips the blankets. When she bucks toward me, I slide in another finger, and her breathing grows louder, rougher.

I continue to finger her as I lower my mouth between her legs. I stroke her with my tongue until she jerks her head away from me and cries out.

There. That's it.

And I've only just gotten started.

Chapter 20

Kim

WHEN I FIRST SAW Max back in June, he looked like the sort of buttoned-up guy that I delight in unbuttoning. And when he growled—actually growled—earlier, it was pretty damn hot. That sound vibrated in my core.

Now, I get to enjoy the sight of him between my legs. He licks me as the orgasm lingers in my body, and it feels incredible. When it comes to oral sex, Max needs no instruction.

I wonder if what happened last time was partly my fault. I should have been clearer about my needs; he would have taken it in stride. I hardly knew him, though, and couldn't have been sure how he'd react.

But we've met a bunch of times now, and anything he learns about my body tonight, he can put to use at a later date. It's hard to think beyond tonight and tomorrow morning, but maybe this can last beyond the weekend.

The dress, bunched around my waist, is annoying me. I sit up just enough to whip it off, and then I keep myself propped up on my elbows so I can watch him go down on me.

Yep, watching Max eat me out is utterly delicious. The view is doing nearly as much for me as his tongue on my pussy—and that's saying something.

I grab his hair, needing to feel him with my fingers, but then my other arm starts shaking. I collapse onto my back and close my eyes. I'm a filthy slut who loves having her pussy licked and filled and will take it any way she can.

Yes. I love feeling like this.

I squirm against his face, and the next time his tongue touches my clit, I teeter on the edge of another orgasm.

"Max," I plead, and he dips his tongue inside me as his finger brushes my clit.

I combust once more.

"Good girl." He has that stern schoolteacher thing going on, and it really works for me.

He crawls up my body, his lips wet with my moisture—it's a fucking beautiful sight. I pull him down and kiss him, working his shirt up his chest as our mouths are fused together. I lean back just long enough to get the shirt over his head, and then my fingers hurry down to unbutton and unzip his pants.

He helps me remove the rest of his clothes before pressing his naked body to mine. I start humping his leg; I'm sure he can feel how wet I am.

He hisses out a breath as I reach for his cock.

"I want you inside me," I say. "Now."

"You're very greedy, Kimberly," he murmurs.

I love when he says my name like that.

He rolls on a condom, and just when I think he's going to slide inside me, he turns me onto my stomach. Max intends to fuck me from behind, and yeah, that'll work for me.

He rubs the length of his sheathed cock over my pussy lips. I groan, desperate for him to penetrate me. I don't need to come again; I just need to feel him.

"Max," I plead.

His low laughter—unlike anything I've heard from him in public—tickles my ear. I clench my inner muscles as he rubs himself against me again.

And then he's fully seated in one powerful stroke, and I nearly weep.

He thrusts in and out. I press my cheek against the bed, grip the sheets in my hands, and let him take me. When he slows down, I howl in frustration, and he spanks me.

"*Ohh.*" The slight sting on my ass makes me feel more present in my body.

"You like that, don't you?"

"Yes." It comes out as a sob because he's fucking me rough and hard now. I feel like a vessel for him to use. I know that's not the truth, I know he cares very much about showing me a good time, but I like feeling as if I'm just here for his pleasure. Paradoxically, that helps me get off.

When he speeds up and bends over so his breath is hot on my neck, I smile. He's going to come any second now, and it's because of me...and when he falls over the edge, I do, too.

This time, he doesn't go to sleep afterward. Once we both use the washroom, we return to bed and lie naked together. He strokes a hand down my back.

"Was that better?" he asks.

"You couldn't tell?"

"It definitely sounded like it was better for you, but I want to be sure."

"It was really good, yeah."

Was it the absolute best I've had? Not quite, but I certainly enjoyed myself. For the first time since last September, I've had satisfying sex. I twist my body this way and that, a dopey smile on my face.

There's nothing quite like a good fuck.

He pulls me against him so my head is resting on his shoulder. After having sex with someone I don't know well, this moment is often awkward, but it doesn't feel awkward now. Being lazy and naked in bed together with him...it's comfortable.

"Any advice for next time?" he asks.

"You should let me suck your cock. I'm very good at it."

His lips quirk, but his eyes darken. "I imagine you are. Everything you do to me...it feels wonderful."

"I'm slutty and I've had lots of practice."

It's clear that Max has no idea how to respond.

"I like being slutty," I say. "Enjoying myself. You can call me that too, you know. When we're in bed together."

The thought of this guy, who hid behind a shrub at Mirabel's wedding in attempt to avoid my notice, calling me a slut—yeah, that turns me on. The fact that he's rather proper and shy? It makes it even more gratifying when he says certain words.

"Noted." He runs his fingers over my shoulder, then down to my inner thigh.

Is this man ready to go again? So quickly?

He laughs softly at my surprise. "I can't perform this soon, but I can touch you. Go down on you. I'm more than happy to do so, if you're interested."

"I'm impressed by your devotion." For some reason, I sound sarcastic, but I mean it honestly.

I move his hand between my legs, and he strokes his fingers through my folds.

I think tonight will pass in a haze of orgasms, and I, for one, am very much looking forward to that.

I watch as Max makes us coffee and breakfast. I'm used to morning afters, but not the kind where the guy takes care of me. He even hummed as he started the coffeemaker; I'm sure he wasn't aware he was doing it. I was afraid to mention it, in case he stopped.

When I look at him now—in khakis, a polo shirt, and glasses—it's hard to believe that this is the man who fucked me hard not half an hour ago.

I feel like I'm in on some delicious secret. He really can be quite naughty in bed.

I'm also amused that he adds a generous spoonful of sugar to his coffee. Apparently, that double-double he ordered at Tim Hortons wasn't a hangover anomaly.

"I really thought you'd take your coffee black," I say.

"Why?" He frowns. "It tastes better with milk and sugar, and it's not as if I'm drinking ten cups of coffee a day. That would be a lot of sugar."

"I don't know. You seem like the kind of guy who'd refrain from eating things that taste good, or doing things that are fun."

"That's really your impression of me?" He opens the fridge. "After the past twenty-four hours, in which I ate my favorite pie with ice cream—"

"Strawberry-rhubarb is your favorite? I had no idea."

"—and had a good deal of sex and wine. That was downright hedonistic of me."

I crack up at Max using the word "hedonistic" to describe himself.

He shoots me a stern look that makes my panties wet, even if I've been awake for only an hour and have already had an orgasm.

I suspect he knows exactly what he's doing.

He didn't seem to know what he was doing the first night we spent together, but now, I feel like I judged him too harshly. He was flustered, and he was right when he told me later that a one-night stand didn't play to his strengths.

Last night and this morning are proof of that.

And I can have more of that sex. He made it clear that a relationship is what he ultimately wants...unless he's changed his mind about what he wants with me.

There's an odd quiver in my stomach. I don't like feeling so unsure of myself. What if he's decided I'm not relationship material? I doubt he'd be keen on a friends-with-benefits situation, and if I'm honest, I don't want that, either—not with him.

He notices that something's up. "What's wrong?"

When Max asks a question, it feels like he really wants to know; he doesn't just want me to brush it off and move on, even if the topic is a bit awkward.

"Do you...do you want to go on another date?" I ask.

"Of course. I'd like to take you out next time, if that's okay? Maybe next weekend?"

I can't help grinning. "Yes, that would be great."

The corners of his lips turn upward.

Huh. This is going remarkably well. Why did I swear off relationships?

As I pour myself some coffee at work on Monday morning, I can't help recalling the way Max hummed as he made coffee in his kitchen. I smile.

"Whatcha thinking about?" Iris asks, walking over with a smirk on her face. "You look awful happy for this time of the week. Have a good date?"

"You went on a *date*?"

Suddenly, Tessa is here, too.

"Uh, yeah," I say.

"With who?"

I didn't tell Iris last week, but now, it feels hard to keep it to myself. "Max Mok."

Iris's eyes widen.

"I knew it!" Tessa says. If we weren't at the office, she'd probably have an even more effusive response. "You acted like nothing was happening, but I *knew* it."

Iris raises an eyebrow. I bet she has questions, but she won't ask them in front of Tessa. "So, Max is the guy giving you that mushy expression?"

"Yeah, I guess he is."

The conversation soon turns to work, but the same cannot be said of my thoughts. Max pops into my mind on a regular basis. I'm not used to mooning over a guy, but here I am.

It's kind of nice.

When I get back to my apartment on Monday after working out, I head to the washroom, where I strip off my dress and underwear, memories of Max undressing me running through my mind. My skin feels flushed and sensitized. I shiver as I think of the way his gaze raked over me.

After showering, I take his food out of the fridge. He cooked extra on Saturday night and insisted I take it home. I don't think this is a regular part of a first date. I got the sense that he was trying to take care of me, and I appreciate it.

Before I can put the food in the microwave, my mother calls.

"Wah, did you know about this?" she asks.

I sigh. "Know about what?" *How can I answer if I don't know what you're talking about?*

"Freddie and his girlfriend broke up! I told him to bring her for Thanksgiving—he can't use the excuse of snowboard season in October—and I'd send money for her ticket. I said I wouldn't take no for an answer. And he said they'd broken up, but he hadn't told me yet because he didn't want to upset me. Do I sound upset?"

I wonder why Freddie decided to end his lie. Perhaps Mom's insistence that they come for Thanksgiving was starting to scare him. Perhaps he was afraid she'd fly out to B.C. for a visit without warning, just so she could meet this so-called girlfriend.

"How could she do this to him?" Mom wails.

"Are you sure she dumped him, not the other way around?"

"Yes, he told me."

Way to go, Freddie. Pinning the demise of your fake relationship on your fake girlfriend.

"I don't understand," Mom says. "How could someone break up with *him*?"

This is the perfect illustration of the difference in how she treats us. If my boyfriend dumped me, she would blame me, not him, no matter what I said. But Freddie? No, he couldn't possibly be at fault.

I can't help feeling resentful that I did the "right" thing—earned a couple of degrees and got a job that's considered respectable to people like our parents—yet I'm the one who can never do right in my mother's eyes. Familiar frustration boils inside me.

A small part of me is tempted to rat Freddie out to my mother. Tell her that he never had a girlfriend. But even if my brother and I aren't close, I'd never do that. Besides, Mom probably wouldn't believe me. Her beloved son faking a relationship? No way.

"I'll have to find someone for him," Mom says.

"I'm sure Freddie can manage by himself."

"I know people in Vancouver."

This leads to a long monologue about who she knows in Vancouver and which of them have appropriate daughters for Freddie. One young woman is considered an option until my mother remembers that she was "a little wild" in university and dyed her hair blue.

"What about you?" Mom asks. "Have you seen Max?"

I can't help laughing. If only my mom knew what I was doing on Saturday night!

But I'm not even going to tell her that I had a date. If Max and I are still seeing each other at Carl's wedding—just under a month from now—I'll say something. I think that's a reasonable amount of time to wait.

"No," I say.

"Aiyah! You don't have all the time in the world—"

"I'm not a package of meat at the grocery store. I don't have an expiration date."

"Do you know what I heard? Sometimes, if the meat hasn't sold, they put on stickers with a new expiration date—"

"Fascinating."

"Why are you being sarcastic? I'm telling you something important. Yes, a woman can get married at any age, but if you want children, you *do* have an expiration date."

"Look, Mom, can we not do this right now? I'm aware that fertility declines with age and menopause is a thing—you've told me before."

She clucks her tongue. "I just don't want you to miss this opportunity."

I decide to placate her a little. "Max and I have been texting. I have everything under control."

"What did he say?"

"We're not talking about this anymore, okay? I don't want my family involved in my dating life. The fact that Gladys had us all sitting at the same table at the wedding—that really was a bit much."

"Why? It's important for families to get to know each other."

"But not so early on."

"I think Gladys believes she's better than me. All three kids getting married this year? She hasn't said so, but I can tell."

It takes another twenty minutes to get my mother off the phone. When I finally end the call, I rub my forehead and close my eyes. I need a moment. Dealing with my mother can be draining. And now I'm actually dating someone, and if it progresses, I'll have another mother to deal with.

Why am I setting myself up for this?

I can't just tell myself that we've only been on one date and I shouldn't worry about it yet...because I've already met his freaking mom. True, she was nothing like my mother, nothing like Troy's mother. But she's probably different when she's not at a wedding banquet.

It's the last thing I need.

I've heard so many horror stories about in-laws over the years, but a lot of my hesitation is based on my own experience. Troy's mom intruded in our relationship and made me feel like I wasn't treating her son properly.

I've never felt like a man's priority—not even close. Never felt like, if his mom did something terrible and made completely unreasonable demands of me, that he'd stand up for me rather than side with her.

It would be better to cut my losses early, right?

Except I don't want to. I'm looking forward to seeing Max again, and when I think of Isobel's wedding, of how he tried to make that situation the best he could for me, I can't help wondering if he's different.

But the bar is so depressingly low, and I feel more uneasy than I did earlier.

I don't know what I'm doing. I'm not the woman I was the last time I attempted to start a relationship.

Am I making a big mistake? How will this end?

Chapter 21

Max

OF ALL MY BROTHERS, Evan is the one who struggled the most with isolation during the pandemic. Leo and I don't mind spending a lot of time at home by ourselves. Jon, to be honest, I don't understand very well. I never have.

But Evan, I get, even if we're quite different. He's a pleasantly social person, and he really missed that—Zoom calls just aren't the same for him. He also got COVID-19 right at the beginning, in March 2020, and while he was still lucky compared to some people, I know it took many months for him to feel like himself again. The fact that his girlfriend of two years dumped him just before the pandemic didn't help matters, either.

Evan, like me, is a relationship person. He's not interested in casual dating or sleeping around, but unfortunately, people keep breaking his heart. I know he's tired and cynical, and I also know that he hates being that way because it's not in his nature.

I invite him over on Thursday and tell him that I'll cook. He's doing better now, but I'm somewhat concerned about him eating enough, although I don't actually say as much.

"So," I say as we sit down to stir-fried beef with black bean sauce, "I had a date with Kim on Saturday."

"You did?" His face splits into a grin. "Does anyone else know?"

"No, and I'm keeping it that way for now." I told Kim that I wouldn't say anything to my parents, but I need advice, and Evan is good at keeping secrets.

"Did it go well?" he asks. "Better than the first night?"

"Much better. I'm seeing her again this weekend, but I'm not sure where to take her."

"You could invite her back here and cook." He gestures to the food. "This is very good."

"That's what I did last weekend. This time, we're going out, but I haven't taken a woman on a date for a while. Two of the places I like closed down during the pandemic."

"There are lots of great patios now."

I make a face. "Many are right by the road and you feel like you're sitting in traffic."

"But they're not all like that."

No, but the ones that come to mind still aren't good enough.

Perhaps I shouldn't be obsessing over this, but I want something really nice for Kim, though not something that says I'm trying *too* hard.

"Any suggestions?" I ask.

"There's a place in Little Italy with a really nice backyard patio."

Okay, that sounds good. "What about the food?"

"It's up to your standards," Evan says with a laugh. "You think I'd suggest a place that's all flash and no substance?"

It's not like my standards are crazily high, but good food is a must.

He tells me the name of the restaurant, and I make a mental note to look it up later. Hopefully it's not all booked up for Saturday—it sounds like the patio isn't too big.

"I'm glad it's going well," Evan says, "even if the start was rather rocky. Not to mention what happened at Isobel's wedding."

"It didn't completely scare her off, which is the most I could ask for." I pause. "She's had bad experiences with boyfriends' families in the past, so I'm counting on you all to behave yourselves."

"I can't speak for everyone else," Evan says, "but I think I can manage. Are you going to Carl and Yvonne's wedding together?"

"I'm not planning that far in advance."

He raises his eyebrows over his cup of tea. I am, after all, a bit of a planner.

"I'd be happy to," I say, "but I'm not sure about her. If we don't end up sitting together for dinner, that's fine. Though I should ask Carl to ensure we're not at a table with all of our parents. I don't need a repeat of that."

Alas, I'm not certain my cousin has anything to do with the planning of his own wedding. He probably left it up to his fiancée and mother.

When Evan gets ready to head out, I make sure he takes some food.

"Oh, I forgot to mention," he says. "I started some new antidepressants, and I think they're working. It hasn't been long, but they seem to be doing something."

"I'm glad to hear it."

"The only problem is..." He shakes his head. "Never mind."

"Side effects?"

He nods but doesn't elaborate.

"I hope they're manageable," I say.

"We'll see. I'm just happy to have found something that actually has an impact."

After Evan leaves, I look up the restaurant he suggested. It appears promising, so I try to make an online booking, but it doesn't allow you to specify whether you want a table inside or on the patio. Hmph.

I don't enjoy making phone calls, but I do it, my pulse speeding up as I listen to the phone ring. Fortunately, I'm able to make a reservation for the patio. Six o'clock—a little earlier than I'd like, but not bad.

After I end the call, it occurs to me that I should have checked the weather first. I breathe out a sigh of relief when I see it's not supposed to rain on Saturday.

I hope that doesn't change.

Chapter 22

Kim

ALL WEEK, I'VE ALTERNATED between being uneasy and excited about seeing Max again.

One moment, I'll think of his long body, covered only by a loose sheet pushed down to his waist, and the way he put on his glasses before getting dressed on Sunday morning. I've never had a thing for a naked guy wearing glasses before, but that definitely did it for me. Whenever I think about him in bed, there's a flutter in my stomach, accompanied by an ache between my legs. I also remember the way he said "hedonistic" and "Kimberly"—both were positively devastating.

Then the next moment, I'll try to think more than a week into the future, and I'll feel a creeping sense of dread about the whole thing. Don't I know better than to get involved with a guy? A guy who doesn't just want something casual?

This stupid cycle repeats itself over and over, and Friday, when I'm working from home, I struggle to concentrate. Both numbers and words aren't making sense. When I finally finish a proposal and hit send, I nearly weep with relief.

I shut down my laptop, put on my workout clothes, and head to the gym in my building. I need to burn off my frustration, and I'm not the sort of person who likes to run in the great outdoors; no, I prefer to work out indoors, thank you very much. I like how it's always the same temperature and there aren't any bugs.

I do fifteen minutes of weights before sticking in my head-phones, loading up a pop culture podcast, and claiming my favorite elliptical machine. Moving my body feels even better than it usual does and...

My phone buzzes. I check the display and see a text from Max, which excites me more than it should.

MAX: Hey

ME: Can't talk right now. At the gym.

MAX: That's OK. Just wanted to tell you to meet me at Christie Station at 5:30 tomor-row.

I can't help a silly smile from coming to my face. Then, embarrassed by my reaction over a mere man, I push myself harder. This podcast is forty minutes, but maybe I'll work out a bit longer today. After all, it's not like I have any plans tonight, other than eating sushi and watching a movie.

For a split second, I wonder if I should call off the date, but every cell in my body protests.

No, I can't do that.

Eventually, reality starts to recede. It's just my body...and this machine...and the words in my ear. I focus on my breathing.

Forty-five minutes later, drenched in sweat, I head back to my apartment and jump in the shower. Then I order my sushi, and while I'm waiting for it to arrive, I pick up my phone and look at Max's texts again. He's sent me a link to the restaurant. After my workout, I feel calmer about the whole thing.

Thank you, endorphins.

Everything with him is going to be okay, isn't it? It won't destroy my self-esteem and ruin my life. No reason to freak out.

I start typing a response.

> ME: Sounds good! Looking forward to it.

> ME: What are you doing tonight? Ironing your underwear again?

> MAX: Yes. It's part of my Friday night routine.

> ME: What else is part of your Friday routine? Polishing your silverware?

> MAX: Naturally.

> ME: How positively hedonistic of you.

> MAX: I believe you need to look that word up in the dictionary.

> MAX: Also, you seem strangely obsessed with my underwear.

I laugh. This conversation might not be *that* funny, but it's delightful talking to him like this. I imagine him studiously typing on his phone, the tiniest of smiles playing on his lips.

When I get a message that my sushi is ready, I head down to collect it in the lobby. I text as I eat, sitting at my kitchen table.

ME: What do you do for fun on Fridays, once you've finished with your silverware?

MAX: Reading, usually.

ME: What are you reading now?

MAX: A nonfiction book about linguistics and the internet.

ME: lol

MAX: It's quite interesting.

ME: I'm sure it is.

ME: I don't mean that in a snarky way, but at this time of week, reading nonfiction is the last thing on my mind. My brain is barely capable of intelligent thought, though I can manage podcasts.

ME: It's especially bad this week.

MAX: What happened this week?

Hmm. I don't want to tell him that this thing between us had me a bit twisted up, especially since I'm feeling my post-workout buzz. I don't want to bring myself down.

And these sorts of hesitations are different when you're texting than when you're face to face. A little pause isn't a big deal.

ME: oh just busier than usual at work.

As soon as I type that, I get another text message, but it's not from Max.

FREDDIE: You should come out for a visit sometime.

ME: You want me to come with Mom and Dad?

FREDDIE: No, it'll be more fun if you visit by yourself.

I consider it. I haven't gotten on a plane since 2019, and I only visited Freddie out west once, a number of years ago. It could be fun, and I'd like to get to know my brother better, away from the rest of the family.

ME: I'll check my schedule and see if I can make it there in the next few months.

ME: When does ski/snowboard season start?

FREDDIE: Late November

FREDDIE: So what's happening with Max?

ME: you're as bad as Mom

FREDDIE: nah, I'm just curious. I won't ask if you're marrying him or make comments about your age.

ME: you better not

A moment later, I get a text from my father.

DAD: Our wifi isn't working.

One of the joys of adulthood—not—is playing tech support for your parents. Mind you, that happened even before I was an adult.

My post-workout glow is starting to evaporate. Yep, so much for a relaxing evening. I'm very popular tonight, it seems.

I return to my conversation with Max.

ME: My dad's having trouble with their wifi, so I better start troubleshooting that.

MAX: You have my condolences. I'll make sure you have more fun tomorrow night.

ME: Will you make me polish your silver-ware?

MAX: Yes

ME: And by polish your silverware, do you mean...

MAX: I mean precisely what I wrote, Kimberly.

I actually giggle, the sound filling my quiet apartment, and feel slightly less apprehensive about trying to solve my parents' tech problems.

Yes, I'm rather looking forward to seeing Max Mok again.

And by that, I mean I'm very much looking forward to it.

Chapter 23

Max

To my dismay, when I wake up on Saturday, The Weather Network is calling for rain in the afternoon. Even if it's done raining by six o'clock, what if the patio furniture is wet and we can't sit there?

I tell myself it's not the end of the world. We can eat inside; the food will still be good.

But I'm annoyed that things aren't going as planned. I've never been one of those people who's amazing at going with the flow.

I leave my apartment with lots of time to spare, taking my large black umbrella with me. I put on my face mask before getting on the subway.

When I reach Christie, it's raining. I stand inside as I wait for my date, trying not to scowl too hard at the weather.

"Hey!"

I startle at Kim's voice.

"Sorry," she says. "I didn't mean to scare you."

"It's okay," I mumble. I should have been prepared. I was, after all, waiting for her.

She's wearing dark jeans today. Her ass looks very nice in them, and as she walks out the door of the station, I have an excellent view of it. I suspect that's why she made a point of exiting before me.

I clear my throat and step outside behind her.

"Did you bring your shark umbrella?" I ask.

"No, I returned it to its rightful owner."

I open up my umbrella. "We can share."

The umbrella is a decent size, but if we're both going to remain dry on the walk to College, she'll have to stay quite close to me. It seems silly to be mildly excited about sharing an umbrella, yet I am.

"I apologize in advance," I say. "I selected this restaurant for the patio, and..." I hold one hand outside the umbrella, and rain falls on my palm.

"That's okay. I don't fault you for being unable to control the weather."

"When I looked at the forecast on Thursday, there was no rain."

"Max," she says gently. "Really, it's fine."

I nod briskly and shut my month. I'll try not to worry more than I already have. There isn't a downpour, nor is there any lightning—it could be worse.

"It reminds me of an episode of *Chu's Restaurant*," she says, naming a Canadian sitcom that's been on for a few years, "when...have you seen it?"

"No. I don't like sitcoms."

"Really?"

I wonder if this is equivalent to saying that I hate baby goats. May need to research this later. Perhaps it's a faux pas.

"Is it because you don't like anything fun?" she asks.

"As I believe I've shown you, I do enjoy *fun*," I say, in an excessively serious voice.

"I have no idea what you're talking about."

I narrow my eyes. "Yes, you do."

Her tongue peeks out of her mouth, and she licks her bottom lip.

It's hard to remain completely in control of myself around Kim.

I swallow. "I find most sitcoms painful to watch. They don't help me relax; they just annoy me."

She chuckles. "The characters do too many stupid things?"

"Yes, and in some shows, there's too much embarrassment. I spend most of the time cringing. It's not how I want to spend my free time."

"Are there any you like?"

I think for a moment. "*Derry Girls*."

"*Derry Girls*?" she says incredulously.

"What's wrong with that?"

"Nothing, but if you get annoyed by stupid behavior—well, surely you must find the behavior of the teenage girls stupid at times."

"For some reason, it's tolerable on that show. Perhaps because I relate to Clare."

"The short, anxious lesbian?"

"She's the reasonable one," I say.

"And you see yourself as the voice of reason?"

"Yes. Plus, I relate to the anxious part—not so much the short lesbian part—though I don't wear my anxiety on my sleeve like she does." At least, I try my best not to.

Kim smiles and releases an odd laugh.

"Is something wrong?" I ask.

"You just surprised me, that's all. Not in a bad way. You could play one of the high school students on that show. Some of the actresses are in their thirties, I think."

"Dear God," I mutter. "The last thing I'd willingly do is return to high school."

But I might willingly watch *Chu's Restaurant*, just because the woman I'm seeing suggested it. My brothers have mentioned it before—apparently, I have the same name as one of the main characters. I didn't watch it for them, but maybe for Kim, I'll try an episode or two. I'm curious about the things she likes.

When we reach the restaurant, I tell the hostess that I have a reservation.

"Follow me," she says.

"Are we still sitting on the patio?" I ask. "Given..." I gesture outside.

"If you don't want to, we can move you inside, but our back patio is well covered by umbrellas. As long as the rain isn't really heavy, you won't get wet."

We're shown to a table under a very, very large red umbrella. Kim immediately begins perusing her menu, but I don't open mine. First of all, because I studied the menu thoroughly before coming here, and second of all, because she's wearing a sleeveless purple top that shows off her chest and I can't seem to drag my eyes away from her. When she glances up and notices me looking, I drop my gaze to my menu.

"Don't worry," she says. "I don't mind if you look."

I clear my throat. "I will look. Later. But we should eat now. I mean, order food. So we can eat later." I have lost my ability to speak properly.

We order an appetizer with fresh figs, goat cheese, and prosciutto. It's a combination I haven't had before, and it's delicious. Each component is good by itself, but even better in combination, and the rain falls softly around us as we eat. There aren't many other people on the patio, and it feels like we're in our own little world.

I decide I'm not upset about the rain after all.

After the appetizer, I have tagliatelle ai frutti di mare, and Kim has a pizza bianca with artichokes and a few other things. The service isn't fast, but I don't mind.

"Any dessert?' our server asks after she clears our dishes.

"We'll take a look at the menu," Kim says.

She convinces me to order a brioche con gelato. I admit I'm a little skeptical. It sounds like an ice cream sandwich, something I haven't eaten since I was a teenager—an actual teenager, rather than someone in their thirties who plays a teenager on TV. However, she's quite keen on the idea, so I relent. There are a small number of gelato flavors to choose from; she goes with chocolate, and I choose pistachio.

When our toasted brioche buns and cool gelato arrive, we take different approaches to consuming them. There's a little spoon—I decide this is the best way to eat it. Kim, on the other hand, picks hers up like a regular sandwich and bites into it. Melted gelato trickles down her chin, which doesn't seem to bother her.

It bothers me, however. I'm desperate to lick it off, but instead, I settle for eating my own gelato.

"Is something wrong?" she asks, placing her hand on my leg.

"No. Nothing's wrong."

"Are you sure?"

She rubs circles on the inside of my knee. She's not touching bare skin—I'm wearing pants—but it feels like she is.

"Kimberly," I say sternly, then realize my error.

She likes when I talk to her that way. It turns her on.

I imagine sliding my hand between her legs and finding her slick. It still seems like a miracle that she's here with me. Not because I'm down on myself and think I'm unattractive, but because it's *her*.

And I know she's here because she wants *me*, and I appreciate that. I'm definitely not just a list of acceptable traits in her mind.

I firmly remove her hand from my leg and return to scooping up gelato with my tiny spoon. She doesn't touch me again, but she makes a show of slowly licking her lips. I have no doubt that she knows exactly what she's doing.

When the bill arrives, Kim says, "Let's split it."

I'm about to argue, about to say that I should pay because I'm the one who invited her out. But something about the set of her mouth tells me this is important to her and it would be of no benefit to argue—and besides, I don't want to stop her from doing something she feels the need to do.

"Okay," I say.

After paying the bill, we leave our little world under the red umbrella and head back to the street. It isn't raining anymore. Kim loops her arm through mine, and my skin still feels warm and prickly.

"Would you like to come home with me?" I ask. "Or if you prefer, we could have a drink, or—"

"Your place."

Unfortunately, I don't live close to Little Italy. It now seems like a terrible oversight on my part to rent an apartment that isn't five minutes from here. We decide to take the streetcar to College Station, and when I see that it won't arrive for three minutes, I'm more than a little frustrated.

Kim laughs softly at me, and that breathy laugh is hot, too. Dammit.

The transit trip is excruciating. Don't streetcars usually move faster than this? When we slow down for a yellow light, I nearly swear, my hands clenching in my lap. Kim looks amused, and I want to kiss that look off her face, but I'm wearing a mask, plus there are two small children nearby.

From the streetcar, we switch to the subway. When the train comes to a stop in the tunnel, I feel like jumping out of my skin. We're in between stations, and I can't tell from the garbled announcement what's happening.

I just want to see that purple shirt on my floor. Is that too much to ask?

I can't remember the last time I was this crazed with lust, but there's just something about Kim and her easy sexuality. I can't help wanting her again and again. She squeezes my hand, but that's not enough contact to satisfy me—not nearly enough.

Luckily, we start moving a minute later, but we still have several stations to go, and then there's a ten-minute walk.

As soon as we get to my place and remove our shoes, I pin her against the wall and kiss her. I wouldn't have been this rough with her the first night, but now I have a better idea of what she likes. We kiss frantically, each trying to get more, more, more. My hands scramble with her clothes, and I'm a little clumsy as I remove her shirt and bra, but then I have my mouth on her breast, and I groan.

God, she tastes good.

We head to the bedroom, losing the rest of our clothes along the way. We topple onto the bed, our lips separating for a moment, and then she's on top of me. My hands roam all over her body, exploring every gentle curve, before stopping at her nipples. I pluck them to tight peaks.

I can feel her moisture on my thighs, and that makes me even more desperate. I plunge two fingers inside her without warning, and she shudders.

When I remove my fingers from her body and paint her moisture over her stomach, she moans in protest.

I position myself above her, knees on either side of her shoulders.

"Suck me off," I say. "Then I'll touch you."

It feels strange to order her around, but her eyes darken with desire.

I'll definitely do that again.

I grasp the base of my shaft and hold it to her lips. When she takes most of me into her pretty mouth, I let out a string of obscenities that I'd never emit in any other situation.

"Good girl," I say when I have control of myself once more.

She's told me a little of what she enjoys, and the rest, I've been able to figure out. She likes praise, and she likes when I'm a little stern, but she also likes when I come undone.

Fuck, she really is amazing at this. I have to hold myself back from coming down her throat. I do wonder how many men she's sucked off, but I don't feel jealous; I'm the one whose bed she's in now, and I appreciate the fact that she's enjoyed herself in the past. Spread her legs, opened her throat.

She presses her thighs together and squirms while she sucks. I love it.

I hold her hair and push myself a little deeper, forcing her to take more of me. I hardly know who I am in this moment, but God, it feels incredible. She feels incredible. I'm so close...

I pull out with a muttered curse. Next time, maybe I'll ask if she'll swallow, but for today, I shift back down her body. All that smooth skin for me to sully. I hold her gaze, and she nods. A few strokes of my hand are all it takes before I squirt across her belly and breasts.

When I see her painted with the evidence of my orgasm, I feel a moment of doubt. But then she smiles, slow and sensual.

Fuck.

I grab a washcloth and wipe it all off, with a gentleness I didn't show earlier. Then I go to the bathroom and clean myself up before returning to the bedroom.

"You want me to touch you now?" I ask.

She nods, and I slip two fingers inside her again.

She's soaked.

I set my mouth to her clit; she moans into her hands, writhing as though she's lost control of the situation, and that's the way I like it. For now. I'm in charge of her pleasure. She's practically thrashing as I finger-fuck her. I haven't forgotten what she likes, not after she showed me last weekend.

"Yes," she says. "Maaax." She shudders against my face, pussy clenching around my fingers, and comes for me.

Afterward, she snuggles up to me, and I breathe in the coconut scent of her hair. This affection...it feels wrong after the filthy sex we just had, and my doubts return.

"Everything okay?" she asks, lifting her head.

I hesitate as I choose my words. "I've never come on someone like that before. It feels too crude, like I shouldn't enjoy it."

"But you did."

"I did."

It felt as if I'd marked her as mine, however briefly. That was part of why I'd liked it, to be honest—and also because I knew it turned her on.

"You know it doesn't mean anything bad about you," she says. "It doesn't mean you don't respect women. In fact, you treat me very well, and you listen."

"I listen. That's an extremely low bar."

"Yes, but I appreciate that you wanted to learn how to get me off, and you made sure it happened over and over last weekend. If you don't want to do something like this again, we don't have to."

"No, no," I say. "I liked it. It's just a little hard to wrap my head around that."

"Because you're just so proper?"

"Well, yes."

Her laughter is light and lingers in the air, and God, I want to hear that sound again and again. But I don't want to speak too much of the future.

I'm afraid that would scare her.

Chapter 24

Kim

I WAKE UP THE next morning at eight o'clock. I'm surprised Max isn't already awake—he woke up earlier than me last weekend. An unfamiliar warmth fills me as I watch him sleep, as I realize that I can't imagine being intimate with anyone else now, not when I'm falling for him.

When I saw him yesterday, scowling at the rain, annoyed it might affect the day he had planned for me, it made me smile. Then he told me he didn't like sitcoms but identified with Clare from *Derry Girls*.

I know Max isn't what you'd find if you googled the definition of "charming," but the little things he says and does—like sending me leftovers last weekend—charm me.

I look around the room. There's a book about European history on the bedside table. Something that I wouldn't find interesting, but I get the impression he likes learning about a variety of subjects. He never tries to show off his knowledge, though.

Yes, I find everything about this guy charming.

When Max opens his eyes, I cuddle up to him.

"Last night was great," I say.

"It was."

I hesitate. "We can stop using condoms, if it's okay with you. If you've been tested, I mean. You're the only person I've slept with since I went to the doctor in the spring, and everything was clear then. I'm not going to sleep with anyone else now."

"No?"

I shake my head against the pillow. "Nope, just you."

He smiles. "I got tested late last year. Nothing turned up then, and I haven't had sex with anyone else since."

"I have an IUD. Do you trust me to manage birth control?"

"Yes, I trust you. But if you do get pregnant…I'd feel better if we talk about that, however unlikely."

"I wouldn't keep it." We're lucky to live in a place where we still have access to such healthcare. "I'd get an abortion, like I did last time." I tense a little, not a hundred percent sure of how he'll react, but it's best to talk about these things. I wouldn't mention the abortion if this was just casual, though I also wouldn't suggest dispensing with condoms in that case.

Max nods, no judgment in his expression. "When was that?"

I exhale. "I was twenty-four. There was a guy I'd been seeing for a few months…I didn't realize I was pregnant until after we broke up. I never considered keeping it." I shrug.

"Do you want children one day?"

"I'm not sure. I think I would, if the circumstances were right, but it's hard to imagine that happening. I wouldn't set out to do it on my own, but I haven't had a relationship in a long time." I suppose I'm in one now, though. "And so many men leave the bulk of the childcare to their wives or girlfriends, don't act like an equal partner."

"I wouldn't do that," he says, and I believe him.

I prop my head up on my hand. "Do you want kids? You told my mother that you want two, but don't worry, I wasn't counting on your honesty in that conversation."

"I think I'd like one or two. Definitely not four."

"You think you have too many brothers?"

"I wouldn't put it that way, but…" He rubs a hand over his face. "After Jon was born, my mother wasn't well, and she had a two-year-old, a four-year-old, and a seven-year-old to care for, in addition to a newborn."

"And your father?"

"He was the only one working, and he wasn't home enough. When my grandma was visiting, she sat me down and told me to be a good boy, to do my best not to worry my mother. I learned to be very self-sufficient, and I tried to make sure Leo and Evan didn't get into trouble."

Oh, Max. It sounds like he had more responsibility than he should have at a young age, and maybe this explains part of who he is.

I slide my hand into his hair. "If I do have kids, I certainly wouldn't want more than two. I can't imagine getting pregnant that many times."

"Very reasonable. I—"

His phone rings. He answers the call and says a few words before jumping out of bed and pulling on some clothes.

"Shit," he says. "Shit, shit, shit."

I stiffen. I've never heard him swear like this. "What's wrong?"

"My mom's in the lobby."

"Are you serious? Your mother's here?"

"Once a month, she goes grocery shopping at a place near where I live. She always stops by to see me beforehand…I forgot…"

"You *forgot*?" I shriek.

Max seems like the sort of guy who lives by his schedule, whether that's a physical day planner or an app on his phone.

"I know," he says. "I'm very sorry. She'll be here in a few minutes."

Unexpectedly meeting a guy's mother, the morning after we slept together? This is the stuff of my nightmares. I suppose it's good that this won't be my first time meeting her, but...

"Can't you say you're busy?" I ask, but I'm already preparing myself for her visit, pulling on my underwear and jeans, plus the extra shirt I brought in my purse. One that, thankfully, shows less cleavage than what I was wearing last night.

"No. She visits every month at this time. I wouldn't do that to her."

"What if her visit was a complete surprise? Would you still let her in?"

"My mother doesn't do surprise visits unless something is terribly wrong, so yes, I would." He opens his dresser and puts on a pair of socks.

Last night, everything seemed perfect, but now, the reality of a romantic relationship has come crashing down on me. Why couldn't I have started a relationship with a man whose family lives on the either side of the country. Better yet, the world?

"Do you want me to hide in the closet?" I ask.

"What? No. It's a bit embarrassing that my mom is coming over when I have a woman in my apartment, yes, but it's fine. I can handle it."

"What about when your mother tells Auntie Gladys, who tells my parents, and suddenly everyone at Carl and Yvonne's wedding is talking about us?"

"That won't happen."

He's often more of a worrier than I am, but right now, he's the calm one. Though he did swear an uncharacteristic amount, it's me who's freaking out.

He puts his hands on my shoulders. "My mom isn't a gossip. She'll just tell my dad, they'll laugh about it together, that's all. I know it's not ideal, and I am very sorry—I can't believe I forgot—but it'll be okay. No need to hide. I'm not ashamed of you."

If I'd gotten my act together, I could have hurried out of his apartment and taken the stairs, but I doubt there's time for that now.

It's already happening. He's picking his mother over you.

I've heard people say that you should pay attention to how a man treats his mother. A man who loves his mom and takes care of her is supposed to be a good sign. But in my experience, a man who's close to his mother has always been a terrible sign, one that he didn't have space for another woman in his life.

Except Max *should* care more about his mom than me, whom he hasn't known for long. And she visits him one Sunday morning a month—there's nothing wrong with that. I'm seeing red flags where there aren't any. Surely a man can have a close relationship with his mother without them being excessively codependent and lacking any boundaries. Just because I haven't encountered that in a partner doesn't mean it can't exist.

But despite that logical reasoning, I still feel wary. My hands are clammy, and the tightness in my chest refuses to loosen.

"Your shirt's inside out." Max pulls it off—nothing sexy about him removing my clothing this time—turns it around, and puts it on for me again.

There's a knock on the door.

"Come out whenever you're ready." He presses a kiss to my forehead, turns to walk out of the bedroom, then hesitates. "If it would be easier for you, I suppose I could tell her you're feeling under the weather."

"No, I'll be out soon."

He leaves the room, and I pop a mint in my mouth and fix my hair.

This is why relationships aren't worth it.

We talked about some difficult things earlier, but I was managing. I was proud of myself for being able to have those conversations.

I wasn't ready for this, though.

When I hear muffled voices and footsteps, I release a breath, fix a smile on my face, and walk out. Max is making coffee, and his mother is sitting at the table. Her eyebrows shoot up when she sees me, but when she speaks, her voice is calm. Measured.

"Hi, Kim. Nice to see you again." It's hard to get a read on how Lynne actually feels about me. "Max mentioned he had company, but he didn't say it was you."

"I was...getting there," he stammers. The tips of his ears are turning pink, and I'm charmed, despite myself.

"I brought pineapple buns," she says, taking out a bag, "but I didn't know there would be three of us, so there's only two."

Max turns to me. "You can have mine."

"No, no, that's okay." I hold up a hand. "I should be going."

"You have to eat something before you leave."

Hmm. Food and coffee *are* appealing...

I sit down, and he brings over a mug of coffee for me, as well as one for his mom. He returns with a small stack of plates plus a mug for himself.

Well, isn't this a cozy, uncomfortable gathering.

Lynne looks at Max, and I swear her lips twitch.

I can't help thinking of what he told me not half an hour ago. His mother wasn't well after his youngest brother was born—though it wasn't clear whether that was more physical or mental.

I bite into my pineapple bun. "This is really good."

"Sadly, I can't take credit for those," Lynne says. "I bought them at a bakery."

"Well, uh, good choice of bakery."

"Your mother said you're talented in the kitchen?"

"She was exaggerating." Perhaps I shouldn't admit that my mom embellished the truth, but sometimes lies come back to bite you in the ass, so it's best to nip this in the bud.

Besides, I refuse to twist myself in knots to please some man's family. I won't be rude, but I won't attempt to be anyone but myself.

"My cooking skills are subpar," I say. "They don't compare to Max's. And I've never attempted to bake anything."

"Has Max cooked for you?"

"Last weekend, but yesterday, we went out for dinner. He picked a nice restaurant."

Was I supposed to pretend that I didn't see him last night? That I just so happened to have arrived at his apartment this morning?

Lynne doesn't seem scandalized, so that's good, but is she silently judging me? I don't want to care, but I do. I find this extremely nerve-racking, and my hand is shaking on my mug. I can barely deal with my own mother; how the hell am I supposed to also deal with Max's?

I drain the rest of my coffee, pass the remainder of the pineapple bun to Max, and stand up. "Sorry, I really should be going. I have plans. With my friends. For brunch."

"You do?" he asks.

Does he not understand that I'm telling a white lie to get out of this situation?

"Yes, remember I told you last night?" I say, my voice upbeat. "I'm meeting Iris and Tessa, and the restaurant isn't very close, so I really ought to be going. It was nice to see you again, Lynne. Thank you for the pineapple bun."

With that, I hurry to the door, slide my feet into my heels, and go to wait for the elevator. I press the "down" button four times, even though it always bothers me when other people do it; it's not like pressing the button over and over will make it come any faster.

"Come on, you asshole," I mutter, which is obviously a very normal way to speak to an elevator.

I hear a door open, and Max walks down the hallway.

Crap.

"Are you okay?" he asks.

I press the button twice more for good measure. "Just fine."

"You know that won't help it go quicker."

"I know!" I snap. "Sorry, I'm just..."

"It's my fault for springing that on you. I'm sorry."

He's apologized multiple times. I believe him, and that makes my reaction worse.

I scrub my hands over my face. "I'm incapable of acting normally where family is concerned. I'm not sure I can do this."

"What do you mean by 'this'?"

I gesture between us. "A relationship. I just don't know if..."

I trail off as he pulls me close. Some of my doubts dissolve simply from his embrace. I was going to say that I didn't know whether a relationship was worth it, but right now, I feel like it could be, even if I need to occasionally eat breakfast with his mother. It would be worth it to have him.

Of course, if his family is shitty to me and he brushes their unreasonable behavior aside, that would be different, but they've been okay so far, haven't they? I think of earlier this morning—Max has been pretty good at talking about things. We'd be able to figure it out, right?

"What can I do?" he murmurs as he continues to hold me.

I was the one who acted a bit irrationally, yet he's here, asking after me rather than being annoyed at me for hurrying out.

"No need to do anything," I say. "I was rude, leaving so quickly, and I wasn't sure whether I was supposed to lie about last night. Did you want her to think I just came over early to see you?"

The quiet rumble of his laughter vibrates through me. "She wouldn't believe it. No, it was perfectly fine."

The elevator arrives, and Max releases me.

"Give my apologies to your mother," I say. "I'll text you later, okay?"

He nods. "Have fun at brunch."

I laugh as I step into the elevator and hold up a hand in goodbye. But as I head down to the lobby and walk to the station, I feel out of sorts.

Do I want to do this? Can I do it, after so many years of being alone?

Chapter 25

Max

I RETURN TO MY apartment and sit down at the table.

"Kim sends her apologies for leaving so quickly," I tell my mother. "She lost track of time. She doesn't want to be late to meet her friends and…" Does Mom believe that lie? I don't know. "She's had some bad experiences with her boyfriends' mothers in the past. That's why she was a bit flustered."

Mom sips her coffee thoughtfully. "Is that why you switched the name cards at Isobel's wedding so she'd sit next to Leo instead of me?"

"You noticed?"

"Yes." She pauses. "When I realized what Gladys had done with the seating arrangements, I figured she was full of nonsense. I assumed that when she saw you two together, you'd merely been exchanging pleasantries, perhaps asking the way to the washroom. But I guess she knew what she was doing."

"You're admitting Auntie Gladys was right about something?"

Mom chuckles. "But she should *not* have sat us all together."

I nod in agreement.

"Before I forget," she says, "you're still planning to install our new ceiling fans, yes?"

"I can do it on Tuesday."

"It's not a rush—I know you have your own life—but if that works for you, we'll be around."

When my mother leaves twenty minutes later, I pick up my phone and enter her once-a-month Sunday visits into my calendar so this won't happen again. How did I forget? Maybe it's because I've been so preoccupied with Kim lately.

I'm about to set my phone down when it rings in my hand. My brother.

Evan, that is. Leo would never call, just text—and he doesn't do that often. Jon occasionally texts me, with the sole intention of pissing me off. Evan sometimes calls instead of texts because he's the rare Millennial who actually likes talking on the phone.

I sit down on my couch and answer. "Hello."

"How was your date?" he asks.

"Last night went well. Thank you for the restaurant recommendation. The food was excellent, and we were able to eat outside, despite the rain." In fact, it was rather romantic, safe under the umbrella together, just the two of us.

"And this morning—oh, shit, is she still there? I shouldn't have called before noon."

"No, she left. Mom stopped by, Kim kinda freaked out...it was awkward." I pause. "Don't tell anyone else about that, okay? Kim's afraid of gossip."

"Oh, man. I can imagine that was uncomfortable, but it's going fine otherwise?"

"I think so."

I'm not sure I can do this, she said, but she didn't end things.

I appreciate that her fears stem from believing she deserves good things and trying to avoid shitty people. Kim is confident in herself, and I like it—and I like how she knows what she wants in the bedroom.

Shit. I have to stop thinking about that. I'm on the phone with my brother.

"Are you ready for next weekend?" he asks.

"What's next week—oh. Right." I really am losing my damn mind to this woman.

"Is the sex that good?"

"I'm not dignifying that with a response."

But yes, it is.

The next day after dinner, I text Kim.

> ME: I'd ask you on a date next Saturday, but I have to go out of the city for the long weekend. Want to do something during the week instead?

> KIM: Sorry, I'm really busy at work. Where are you going?

> ME: Up north with my family.

> KIM: We'll go out the following weekend.

I don't like the idea of waiting nearly two weeks to see her again, but I can manage. I'm afraid if I push her, she'll run.

Plus, I'm still unsettled that I forgot about my mom's visit. I'm the predictable son, the one she doesn't have to worry about. It wasn't like me; I feel like Kim has made me into someone different, and I'm a bit overwhelmed by my desire to see her all the time.

I also think I'm more vulnerable with her than the women I've dated in the past, like I'm wearing my anxiety on my sleeve, which is unnerving.

This reminds me of Clare from *Derry Girls*, and speaking of sitcoms...

ME: I started Chu's Restaurant.

KIM: Yeah? How many episodes?

ME: I watched five yesterday afternoon.

KIM: Really?? I assumed you were the kind of guy who restricts himself to a single episode at a time and never stays up late watching anything.

ME: Well, I don't stay up late for TV. That would be foolish.

KIM: I'm foolish sometimes. What did you think of the show? If you binged it, you must not have hated it.

ME: It was tolerable.

KIM: High praise

> ME: Better than most sitcoms. Waverly is
> kind of annoying, but I like Paula.

Once again, I identify with the lesbian. Paula is the oldest of three siblings. Rather grumpy, she communicates mainly in grunts. She has a crush on a woman at the brewery but refuses to confess her feelings, too afraid of rejection. Some people might find that silly, but I can relate.

Though it's very different from what happened with Kim. She was the one who approached *me*. But I did eventually ask her out, despite our unimpressive one-night stand and her stance on relationships.

How is she feeling about relationships now?

I don't feel prepared to ask her that, but perhaps I can tell her what I'd like.

> ME: Can I see you sometime next week?
> I come back on Monday afternoon. I could
> visit you that night or the following one?

After I send the text, I rest my head against the back of the couch and sigh. My knee bounces, and I put my palm on it and force myself to be still.

> KIM: Maybe? I'll let you know in a few days.

She didn't say no, which feels like a victory.

ME: I'm on season 2 now.

KIM: What do you think?

ME: I kinda hate Maxwell, even though we have (almost) the same name.

ME: Like, the guy threw a dart at a map to decide where to live. WTF.

KIM: Too much chaos for you?

ME: He needs to learn to make better decisions.

KIM: Aww, I love him! He's very popular.

ME: So I've heard. I do not understand.

KIM: He's easy on the eyes, and people like himbos.

ME: I can't believe that's an actual word.

KIM: Language evolves. It's not static.

ME: I'm aware. But it should evolve in a more sensible fashion.

KIM: If you're worried that I'd leave you for him if I were to, I don't know, bump into him in the street while carrying a cup of taro milk tea...

ME: You've really thought this through.

KIM: Don't worry, I'd still pick you.

ME: I'm on episode 11. Maxwell (I refuse to call him Max) took Waverly on a hike to see a cool tree.

KIM: Do you have something against cool trees?

ME: She wore heels on a hike! Why? I cannot deal with the silly choices these people make. But I like the grandfather and parents.

KIM: Come on, you do silly things too. Like trying to hide behind a potted shrub that was two feet shorter than you.

ME: ...

ME: It was only two inches shorter.

KIM: Ha

ME: I'm not saying the characters are completely unrealistic. I just prefer my fiction to make more sense than reality does most of the time.

By the time I leave the apartment on Friday morning—I'm taking the day off—to pick up Leo for the weekend, I've watched two seasons of *Chu's Restaurant*. I feel like I've lost a few brain cells, though I do want to see the third season.

I'd normally look forward to this trip with my family, but I'll miss seeing Kim—and I'm not sure how strong my signal will be and whether I'll be able to text her much. At least we've now arranged to see each other on Monday.

I wonder how she'll be spending the next few days.

Chapter 26

Kim

I TAKE MY SWEET time getting out of bed on Saturday morning, treating myself to a luxurious masturbation session before starting my day. Three different toys may or may not be involved. I may or may not think about Max fucking me on the counter in the middle of cooking dinner, with no concern for food safety.

Okay, I definitely do that.

After some coffee and toast, I drive to an Asian supermarket that I haven't been to in a while. It's not the closest one to my apartment, but they have some snack foods that I can't get anywhere else.

I've just put a bag of lychees in my shopping cart when I hear a familiar voice speaking in Cantonese. I freeze.

"Fucking hell." I try to be quiet, but an older man cuts me a glare. "Sorry," I whisper, then hurry away with my shopping cart, attempting to avoid the notice of Troy's mom.

This is some rotten luck. The last thing I want to do is have a conversation with my ex-boyfriend's mother, and there's nowhere to hide in the produce section. I hurry away and grab everything else I need before circling back to the produce.

But when I round the corner to the checkout, she's right there.

I start to walk backward. Perhaps I need some meat, or maybe I should check if pineapples are on sale...

"Kim!"

Too late.

Well, maybe it's not a big deal. It's not as if I'm dating her son anymore. If she doesn't like me, who cares?

"Stand behind me," she says. "This lane is moving the fastest."

That's not so bad, is it?

But then she looks at my shopping cart, and I can see her judging my choices. There are probably too many snacks and noodle bowls for her liking.

She clucks her tongue. "Troy said you didn't do much cooking. I can see that hasn't changed."

"Yeah, I'm busy."

"How old are you now? Thirty-two?"

I'm not sure my own father knows my age, but Troy's mother remembers.

"That's right," I say.

"You need to eat well to keep your figure as you get older."

"I'll keep that in mind." Though I try not to sound *too* sarcastic, she narrows her eyes at me nonetheless. I'm not very tall, but she's shorter—five feet at the most—yet I still find her a bit intimidating. I don't want to, but I do.

"He's engaged, you know," she says, and I swear she lifts her nose in the air.

Her words shouldn't bother me. It's not like I still have feelings for Troy—God, no—but I feel the tiniest bit of discomfort that he's "ahead" of me.

"Give him my congratulations," I tell her, keeping my tone light.

"That could have been you, if only you hadn't broken his heart."

She's acting so superior, but I'm the one who's too good for Troy, the guy who'd go running to his mother when I didn't do what he wanted.

"I have no regrets," I say simply.

Her mouth drops open. I guess I was supposed to say "if only" and act like he was the one that got away.

"Why should I?" I ask. "He's apparently happy, and I have a boyfriend."

It's the first time I've called Max my boyfriend, and the word feels awkward on my lips. When faced with my ex's mother, the idea of having a boyfriend makes me uncomfortable.

But I press on. "He's a respectable engineer and my mother loves him."

Her eyes widen. I bet she's surprised that someone like Max would dare date a mouthy woman like me, but then it's her turn at the checkout. I consider moving to another line, but she was right about one thing—this is the best lane, and I don't want to change lanes just to get away from her.

As I drive home, my mind is filled with memories of what that last relationship did to me. Made me feel like I was always the problem, like I never did enough, which is why I swore I'd never put myself in that position again.

Yet here I am.

When I get to my apartment, I put away my groceries, open up a bag of Turtle Chips, and waste time on my phone. Losing myself in some online drama sounds appealing right now. I go to advice forums and read about people with even more fucked-up family situations than me. Some of the stories are probably creative writing exercises, possibly rage bait, but I don't care as long as they're entertaining. The ones about men who ask for open marriages, then get mad when lots of people want to sleep with their wives—and their wives have a great time!—are some of my favorites.

I also find an argument over whether you should wash your rice, which soon devolves into "washing rice is racist" and "not washing rice is racist" and someone saying Asian people who don't own rice cookers must hate themselves.

Sure, my blood pressure is rising, but at least it has nothing to do with my own life.

As entertaining as this is, I don't want to stay here all day, scarfing Turtle Chips—huh, will you look at that, I'm almost finished the bag—so I text Iris and ask if she's free. (Tessa went to her hometown with Malcolm for the August long weekend.) Iris replies that she'd be happy to see me, and I suggest a cider bar on Ossington that I've been meaning to try.

I want to look hot tonight, so when it's time to get ready, I put on the jeans I wore last weekend—the ones that made Max stare at my ass—as well as a clingy black top. I'm in the mood for some dramatic makeup, so I spend more time on it than usual, recalling that Troy said he preferred a more natural look.

Well, fuck Troy. Besides, he had no idea when I was wearing makeup and when I wasn't.

When I'm finished, I look pretty damn good, if I do say so myself, and I can't help imagining Max's reaction. He's not in the city, but I snap a picture in the mirror and send it to him. He doesn't immediately respond, but he's with his family and his signal might be questionable this weekend, so that doesn't bother me. He'll see it when he sees it.

The cider place is busier than I expected, but Iris has managed to snag a spot on the backyard patio.

"Hey," she says. "You look amazing."

I scan the QR code to bring up the list of ciders on draft, and I soon make my decision. The server brings my cider over quickly, and I immediately chug half of it, barely tasting it, though it's refreshing after walking from the subway station in this hot weather.

Iris raises her eyebrows. "What's up?"

No sense in pretending nothing's wrong. "I saw Troy's mom at the grocery store."

Now that I say it aloud, it sounds stupid, and I'm pissed that it's affected me so much.

"You mean the woman who made your life a living hell? Who called you at midnight to yell at you because you didn't do his laundry, and hired a private investigator—"

"Yeah, that's the one." I didn't know Iris back then, but she's heard stories. I take another healthy swallow of my drink and tell her about our exchange.

"Well, good luck to his fiancée." She raises her glass.

"Yeah, good luck to her." Maybe Troy will decide he wants to sleep around, insist they open up their marriage, and she'll be the one enjoying the sex of her life while he argues about rice cookers online.

The thought shouldn't make me gleeful, but it does.

"How do you deal with Alex's mom?" I ask Iris.

"She died before we met."

"Shit. I'm sorry. I forgot about that." I pause. "What about the rest of his family?"

"His dad and brother? We get along fine." She leans forward. "How's it going with Max? Is the sex good? I assume it must have gotten better after the first time."

"Yeah, much better."

If she notices me blushing, I'll blame it on the alcohol. I don't normally blush over a little sex talk, but when I think of Max fucking my mouth...

I clear my throat. "But I saw his mother again last weekend. He forgot she was visiting that morning."

"Did he try to hide you in the closet?"

"Nah. It went okay, I guess."

I can't imagine Lynne judging my purchases and telling me to watch my figure at the grocery store, but I don't know her well, and the events of the past week have me unsettled.

Fortunately, Iris changes the topic. Her grandmother's birthday is coming up, and apparently, she wants a "big bash," so we talk about that for a while before I head to the washroom. On the way back to the patio, I stop to look at the food specials on the chalkboard behind the bar. I don't remember those in the online menu, but maybe they were there—I was more focused on the drinks than the food when I looked at it.

"Hey."

I turn my head and see a white guy wearing an easy smile and a black dress shirt.

"Hi," I squeak, uncharacteristically frazzled. When an attractive guy says hello to me at a bar, I'm usually more on my game. And this guy is attractive, but I don't *feel* anything.

I don't feel any lust, I mean.

"I have a boyfriend." I say the words in a rush. "Really, I do, I'm not lying." Then I make my escape to the patio, where I immediately pull up the drinks menu and consider what to get next. It's a bit hard when my eyes are barely making sense of the words, though.

One-night stands and casual sex would be so much easier. Yes, you have to be careful about your safety, but emotionally, they're simpler. Your lives don't get tangled together. You don't look forward to every little conversation. You don't obsessively check your phone to see if he saw the photo you sent him earlier.

I wish I could go back to being the woman I was a few months ago. I don't like feeling this torn up inside. I think of Max texting me about *Chu's Restaurant*...and I turn warm and gooey.

These sorts of feelings are dangerous. They make you put up with nonsense that you shouldn't tolerate, all in the name of love.

Iris leans forward and touches my wrist. "Are you okay?"

"I'm fine. Just fine."

She sees straight through that lie. "I once thought long-term relationships were miserable and never wanted that for myself. But I met the right person—and realized the truth about the marriages in my family—and that changed."

I'm not Iris, though. I'm not sure that's possible for me.

My phone buzzes. I take a quick peek.

Very nice, Max says. Your tits look great in that top.

I love when he's a little vulgar, and I know he's using that language because he's aware I like it, which is...

Yeah, I'd definitely rather sleep with him than a random dude I met at a bar.

Save that thought for later, I type. Can't wait to see you when you get back.

I put my phone away and return my attention to Iris. But at the back of my mind, I can't help wishing that I hadn't made my life so damn complicated.

Chapter 27

Max

The detective is the murderer. I'm almost positive. But—

"Hey, Max," Jon says cheerfully, approaching the lake in his swim trunks, towel slung over his shoulders. "Whatcha doing?"

"What does it look like I'm doing?" There's a book in my hand. It's pretty obvious.

On the Muskoka chair next to me, Leo—who's been doodling—chuckles.

Jon grabs my book. He's always cared more about annoying me than anyone else, for some mysterious reason. "I read this one."

"I wasn't aware that you knew how to read."

He barks out a laugh. "I'll leave you to it." And with that, he tosses the book on my lap, sets his towel on the dock, and jumps in the lake.

I'm just glad he didn't spoil the ending for me. He did that once, years ago, and I haven't forgiven him.

I return my attention to the page, and my suspicions about the murderer are soon confirmed. When I finish the book, Jon is still in the water, Leo is dozing beside me, and the sun is partially hidden by the clouds.

It's a beautiful day out here, and I'd normally enjoy this weekend with my family more—Jon's occasional attempts to disrupt my peace notwithstanding—but I can't help thinking about seeing Kim again.

I pull out my phone and look at the photo she sent me last night. Her lips are painted red, and she's blowing a kiss at the mirror. I've never had a girlfriend who sent me pictures like this before. I jerked off in the shower last night, and when I woke up this morning, I was thinking about her again. She consumes an unnerving amount of my thoughts and all of my fantasies. It's been over a week since I've seen her, and I need to touch her. A week is far too long when it comes to Kimberly Sung—hell, even a day or two feels like too long. I can hardly wait until tomorrow.

I imagine waking up with her in my bed every day. That sounds like perfection.

And I imagine, next year, bringing her on a family vacation.

This is my first time in Kim's apartment; however, it's hard to care about that when she's right in front of me, wearing a pair of itty-bitty jean shorts as well as a tight tank top.

God. This woman.

"You like my outfit?" She twirls around, giving me a good view of her ass.

"Yeah." I pull her close. "I missed you."

I say those words without thinking, and when I look into her eyes afterward, I wonder if that was a mistake.

"Are you okay?" I murmur.

"I will be," she says, light and flirty, "once you're inside me."

I push her against the wall, rattling a picture frame, and kiss her. She wraps a leg around my hips and tries to climb me.

I never feel as out of control as I do around her. Being with Kim makes me feel alive in a way that nothing else ever has.

As soon as she removes my shirt, I slide my hand into her shorts, needing to touch her. I slip a finger into her moisture and hiss out a breath.

"A man hit on me at the bar," she says.

I freeze. "And?"

"I told him I have a boyfriend."

Hearing her say that word—it ratchets up the heat in my body even further, which shouldn't be possible.

I kiss her hard. By some miracle, this woman is *mine*, and I'm going to make her feel as good as I possibly can.

She moans in protest as I remove my hand from her panties. I make quick work of her clothes, tossing them in a pile on the floor. Then I push her to her knees, take out my hardening cock, and hold it to her lips.

"That's a good girl." I stroke her hair as she takes me deeper. I know my words will make her even wetter, and nothing could please me more than turning her on.

When I'm perilously close to losing it, I pick her up and carry her to the bedroom, setting her down on the blue duvet. She's flushed and squirming and beautiful, and after our first night, I never would have imagined she'd be like this for me. It feels like an impossible gift.

"No condoms today?" I want to be sure before we go any further.

She nods in response.

Being inside her, with nothing between us...I think that might be the end of me.

I lick her pussy, circling my tongue around her throbbing clit, and her back bows off the bed. The taste of her drives me wild. I keep devouring her until I can sense the tension building in her body, and then I ease back.

"Fuck you." She's never shied away from swear words, not from the very first moment I met her.

I chuckle, low and rough, before taking mercy on Kim. I touch her just the way she likes and lick her with abandon. When she comes, her lips part, and it's unspeakably gorgeous.

I shed the rest of my clothes and slide all the way inside her as she's still shuddering. She sobs and twists her head to the side; I touch her cheek and turn her to look at me.

"Hey," I whisper, holding myself still.

"Hey."

The pure pleasure of being inside her like this, of gazing into her eyes, has me reeling. For a moment, it's like time comes to a halt. Then I pull out and thrust back into her, and she cries out as she comes again.

I hold my hips still once more, waiting for her to recover, and press kisses all over her face and neck and shoulders. I'm already so, so close.

"Please," she murmurs, and I start moving again. Right now, she can barely form words, and I'm the one who did that to her.

I feel like I'm on the glass floor in the CN Tower. I don't normally experience vertigo, but I did when I stood on that glass floor, and it completely caught me off guard.

My feelings—they're chaos.

But I keep moving within her, kissing her, touching her, and that grounds me just enough to prevent me from spinning out of control.

I take her nipple into my mouth. How did I not do this the first time we were together? It's one of my favorite things now, pulling that bud between my teeth. She makes a noise that sounds like "ungaah" and grips my hair.

I slide a hand under her ass; she wraps her leg around me as we move together, perfectly in time. I want this to go on forever, but I won't last much longer.

"I'm almost..." I say. "Can I...?"

"Yes," she groans.

I lick my finger and touch her clit. I can tell she's about to come again, any second...and then my own orgasm hits and I pour myself inside her as she shakes beneath me.

"Fuuuck," I growl.

I hold her as our pleasure ebbs, pressing a long, slow kiss to her lips. I'm utterly undone; anything more would require too much coordination.

Kim grabs a towel from the bedside table and slides it underneath her hips. I kneel back and admire the mess I made. I love knowing that *I* did this to her, that she let me spill myself inside her body.

She trails her fingertips over her folds, and fuck, that's hot. She dips two fingers inside her channel, then slides them into her mouth, holding my gaze the whole time. If my body were capable of it right now, I'd be hard again.

She touches herself once more and paints her inner thigh with my cum.

Filthy. That's how she described herself.

"Can I clean you up?" I ask.

A crooked smile graces her face. A soon as I have her permission, I bury my face between her legs, and it doesn't take long before she's twisting in the sheets, unable to control herself again.

She goes to the washroom, and then I take my turn. When I come back to bed, she looks completely drugged out on sex.

I feel a strange sense of pride at seeing her like this, and at the same time, I'm unmoored. Like I'm so far from my normal, controlled self, in uncharted waters—but I wouldn't change a thing. I try not to show just how chaotic my feelings are, and I hope I succeed.

Because if Kim figures out that I love her, I'm afraid it'll scare her, and right now, she's blissfully content. She curls up against my side, and this time, she's the one who falls asleep in minutes, whereas I'm wide awake, even if I can barely move my limbs.

I shouldn't feel so strongly about her already. Never before have I considered saying "I love you" to a woman I've known for less than three months. It doesn't make sense. It's something that takes time, but as I feel her breathe against me, I know it's the truth. Though I can't explain how it happened, I know what I feel.

She mumbles something in her sleep, and I think she's going to wake up, but I run my hand through her hair and she seems to relax.

Oh, God. I'm so gone for this woman, and I can sense the anxiety building in my veins because I'm not sure she feels the same way.

My phone buzzes, and I check it.

It's my mother, wondering if Kim would like to join us for dinner on Thursday.

Chapter 28

Kim

WHEN I AWAKE, THE late-day sun is slanting through the window, and my body feels well used. Just the way I like it. I stretch this way and that before opening my eyes. Max is looking at something on his phone, but he puts it aside as soon as I sit up.

"Hey," he says. "Have a good nap? You were out for at least an hour."

"Mmm. Yes."

A fuck and a long nap? Yeah, that's my idea of a good time. I'd be happy to repeat the cycle, but when I start kissing Max, he doesn't kiss me back.

"Is something wrong?" I ask.

"No."

That sounds like a lie. I open my mouth to call him on it, then snap my lips shut.

"But my refractory period is more than ninety minutes," he says.

"Fair enough."

"And I also...sometimes when I'm anxious...I can't..."

I frown. "Why are you anxious right now?"

"Work stuff, I guess. Going back to work after taking a four-day weekend."

This feels like it's not the whole truth, but...

He clears his throat. "I used to have a lot of performance anxiety, actually."

"About work or sex?"

"Both." He laughs ruefully. "It was during grad school. Although when it came to school, I was still able to perform, but…"

"Not in the bedroom?"

"It was a brutal cycle because the more trouble I had, the more anxious I got, which meant I had more trouble and…anyway. I had some therapy, which did help. Not being a broke grad student improved my mental health, too. It's okay now, but you should know, in case it happens again."

I nod. I'm not sure what to say, though I don't want him to feel like it's something I wouldn't be able to handle if it becomes an issue in the future.

Yes, I'm thinking about having a future with a man. It scares me, but I try to push those feelings aside.

I press my lips to Max's and hold him close, hoping that says more than whatever words my half-asleep brain could conjure up. I doubt this is the sort of thing he shares often. I'm glad we managed to develop a satisfying sexual relationship after what happened the first night, and I truly believe we'd be able to talk and figure it out if anything changed.

"While you were napping," he says, "my mom texted and asked if you'd like to come over for dinner on Thursday."

"Dinner with your parents?"

"It wouldn't be just us. My brothers would be there, too."

"I don't know."

He runs a hand through my hair. "I said I thought you were busy that night but I'd ask to be sure. I figure the next time we'll see our families—as a couple—will be at the wedding this Saturday. We'll start with that and go from there."

"Sounds like a plan."

I'm thankful he's not pushing me.

I enjoy the intimacy of lying in bed with Max, his idle touches. I wonder how many relationships he's had in the past; I don't feel jealousy, just curiosity.

"Can I ask you something?" I say.

"Go ahead."

"How did your previous relationships end? Have you had many? I told you what happened with me, but I don't know about you."

"I've had a few girlfriends." He looks down at the sheets. "A couple of my exes said I was a bit...closed off. They felt they couldn't fully know me."

Huh. "I've never felt like that with you." In fact, Max has been quite vulnerable with me.

"I'm glad." He pauses. "I broke up with my last girlfriend because I could tell she was settling."

"What do you mean?"

"She was thirty-four and wanted to get married and have kids. She thought I'd be a good husband and father, but I knew she didn't love me, even though we'd been together for two years. I felt bad for ending things, and I doubted my decision for a long time, but I'm glad I did it, for my sake."

Because then I found you.

Though he doesn't say those words, I feel them as he holds my gaze. There's something wonderful and terrifying about it all.

"I'm glad you did, too," I say quietly.

"For a while, I worried that I could only be an acceptable match, and no one could feel strongly for me."

I'm annoyed with this woman for making Max feel that way. He deserves to be with someone who loves him with her whole heart.

Is that me? Can I be what he deserves?

Was the sex so good in part because there were *feelings* involved?

It's been years since I felt this way about anyone, and last time, it didn't end well. I'm not in love with Max yet, but I can tell I'm getting there. I could love him.

"I know you'd never settle, Kim," he says, "and I like that. You're here because you want to be, and you bring out a side of me that no one else ever has."

He kisses me, nice and slow, molding my body against his, and my doubts begin to recede. It's so heavenly to feel his skin against mine. I don't think I could tire of the way that feels, the way he touches me.

"Where are your toys?" he asks.

"Toys?" I feel disoriented.

"Sex toys." Max speaks those words in that serious voice of his, and it's enough to make me wet.

I open my bottom drawer. "Take your pick."

He studies them carefully, lifting each one in turn, and I can barely stand the anticipation. Finally, he selects my smallest flexible dildo.

"I want you to be filled for the rest of the day," he says. "Either with a toy or my cock."

"It's only six thirty."

The corner of his mouth tilts up. "I'm aware." He covers my body with his and teases my pussy with the tip of the toy. "What do you think?"

He slides it all the way inside me, and I groan.

"Yes," I say.

"Good." He nods briskly. "I thought you'd agree."

He leans closer, until his lips are a hair's breadth from my ear. My pulse speeds up as I wait for what he'll do next. I feel like I'm standing on a cliff, my toes curled over the edge, barely hanging on.

"You're a slut, Kimberly," he says at last. "You like to be filled as often as you can, don't you?"

"Yes." I squirm on the bed. "Yes."

He used *that* word, and now I feel like I'm falling.

His expression gives nothing away, but I can see the desire in his eyes. I'm so attuned to him now.

Just then, my stomach growls. How inconvenient.

"We should eat something," I say reluctantly. "I can't cook you anything fancy—"

"I wouldn't expect you to."

"—but we can order something. Or I've got a bunch of eggs..."

"I can make food," he says. "Just tell me what I'm allowed to use in your fridge."

"You really don't—"

"Let me take care of you."

As he says that, it strikes me that I rarely feel *taken care of*. Not by my family, and not in my previous relationships.

Yep, I'm definitely falling.

"Let me take care of you," he repeats, softer this time. "You just stay here, nice and full of cock, okay?"

I agree, helpless when he speaks to me like that. For a moment, I think he's going to reach between my legs and make me come again—it wouldn't take much—but he doesn't.

He gets out of bed and puts on his clothes. "While I'm gone, don't touch yourself. I'm in control of your orgasms tonight."

"Is that so?"

He raises an eyebrow, as if daring me to contradict him, but I know he'd stop if I said I didn't want to follow his rules.

Except I do.

"But in case it becomes too much," he says, "you should pick a safeword."

Yes. That's a good plan.

"Waffles." It's the first thing that comes to mind. Perhaps because I'm hungry.

"Very well. If you can't speak, you can also tap the headboard."

I nod.

"Promise me you'll do that if needed." He strokes my jaw. "I don't want to hurt you."

"I promise."

He puts on his glasses and leaves the room. It's a minute or two before I can even manage to pick up my phone. I check the news, social media...and then I adjust my position and become very *aware* of the toy inside me. I don't touch it, but I clench my inner muscles.

I can definitely feel it—*him*—between my legs, and I love it.

When he returns to the bedroom, he sets a tray with eggs, toast, and a small salad beside me on the bed.

"Thank you." I adjust my position so I can eat, which of course adjusts the position of the dildo, and I release an unsteady breath.

"Everything okay?" His voice is calm, but there's no mistaking the heat in his gaze.

"Yep...just...great."

We eat in silence. He really is a better cook than me—it's obvious even in this simple food, though I can't focus on what I'm eating as much as usual.

Once I set down my fork, he whisks the tray away, and as he walks to the kitchen, I call out, "No need to do dishes."

He ignores me. I can hear him loading up the dishwasher, and I groan in frustration. By the time he returns to the bedroom, I'm desperate for him to touch me.

Max doesn't make me beg. He climbs into bed, not bothering to remove his clothes, and slips his hand between my legs.

"Very wet, I see." He works the toy in and out, brows drawn together in concentration as he focuses on my reactions. He's still wearing his glasses. Then he shifts down the bed and lies in front of me, eating me out in tandem with his thrusts.

I'm shaky and tender and so very needy. The dildo is starting to feel like too much, but I need *more*. I need to come for him. I writhe on the bed, bucking against his face.

Yet as desperate as I am, my orgasm catches me off guard, my cry of ecstasy piercing the silence as I shake.

I'm overwhelmed.

He removes the toy from my pussy, and I almost weep with relief...and then he stuffs it in my mouth.

Fuck.

When I met Max, I hoped he would be naughty in the bedroom, but I certainly didn't imagine *this*.

Hurriedly, he shoves down his fly and takes out his cock, which is now rock hard. He gives it a few pumps before positioning it at my entrance. Even before he pushes inside, I know the truth: I will be utterly wrecked after this, just as he promised. By this man who cooked and cleaned while I lay naked in bed.

He thrusts into me, and I try to cry out, but the dildo muffles the sound.

He removes it and sets it aside. I turn my head and whimper into the pillow, but he puts his hand on my chin and forces me to look at him. He's wearing a goddamn dress shirt and glasses, and honestly, it's too much for me.

"Kimberly," he murmurs.

He pulls out of me just long enough to kick aside his pants and boxer briefs and turn me onto my stomach, and then he's inside me again. Fucking me with deep, insistent strokes, animalistic growls coming from his throat as he smacks my ass.

I'm completely lost to him. I have no idea what's happening, what I'm doing.

I think I come again, but it's hard to know. Everything has become a bit of a blur, but we're joined together—that's the one thing that's crystal clear.

He growls louder and spends himself inside me.

Max doesn't immediately pull out but stays motionless on top of me. When my eyes jolt open, I realize I briefly fell asleep. The tip of his soft cock is still inside my pussy. I moan in satisfaction, but we must be a sticky mess.

He carries me to the shower, where he cleans me up, and as soon as I'm back in bed, he stuffs the dildo inside me again.

He wasn't lying about keeping me full all evening.

"I appreciate that you kept your word," I tell him.

"Of course," he says solemnly.

When he finally removes the toy, two hours later, I literally weep with relief. I've lost track of the number of orgasms I've had, and I'm not sure how I'll be able to move tomorrow, but I feel deliriously good, and I can't help giggling, even as a few tears leak out of my eyes.

"You did so well," he murmurs, stroking my hair, looking at me in wonder.

Yep, I'm utterly wrecked.

I can't sleep.

I blame it on my late nap, which probably threw off my sleep schedule. Also, I've only shared a bed with Max a handful of times, and this is the first time he's been in my apartment. I can't seem to adjust to his presence. He's not snoring and hogging all the space, but it's distracting nonetheless.

But more than anything, it's my mind that's keeping me up. It refuses to stay quiet.

Now that I'm exhausted, no longer in a state of post-orgasmic bliss, my thoughts return to how romantic love hasn't been particularly great to me in the past. When I freed myself from it, I felt like I was taking a positive step for *me*. No longer would I let men—and their families—make me feel as if I wasn't enough. That meeting with Troy's mother reminded me of what I left behind.

Yet I'm walking down that path again. Another man, another family, to make me feel bad about myself.

I roll over. I can still feel Max between my legs, and I think...this relationship has to be worth it. It better be. But wanting something to be true doesn't always make it so.

I awake when my alarm goes off, after a solid three hours of sleep—at most.

"Fucking hell," I mutter.

Then Max pulls me into his arms and I don't feel like swearing any more.

"I didn't sleep well," I say.

"How about you stay here for a few more minutes while I make coffee?"

I mumble my assent and burrow into the pillow.

A while later, I smell coffee, and I blearily open my eyes to see a mug and coaster on my bedside table. Then the mattress shifts, and there's a warm body behind me. I shut my eyes again.

"I love you," he murmurs, and I'm positive he thinks I'm asleep.

For a split second, my whole body smiles, but then my fears from last night, the ones that kept me awake, rush back.

As I continue to feign sleep and let Max stroke my hair, a part of me protests.

He's different.

But of course, none of my past relationships started the way they ended. Is it foolish to think this could be the one to break the pattern?

"I have to leave soon," Max says apologetically. "I need to get home and start work."

I turn over and look at him. He's pressed and perfect, and I'm convinced he's the most handsome man in the world.

"Hey, you," I say.

This man will be my undoing.

Chapter 29

Max

Carl and Yvonne's wedding is quickly approaching, and it feels like a big deal.

Of course, the wedding day is a big deal for my cousin, but it also feels like a big deal for my relationship with Kim. It's the fourth wedding of the year for both of us. The fourth and final wedding.

We're actually together now, and everything seems to be going well. For the most part, anyway. Sure, I occasionally experience vertigo and I'm afraid to confess my love for her—when she's not sleeping, that is—but we see each other regularly and she lets me look after her. And not just in the bedroom, though I'm doing an excellent job there, based on the noises she makes. I think I've made good on the promises I made by the lavender fields.

But somehow—I can't fully explain it—this wedding feels like a test of our relationship.

The morning of the wedding, I'm having breakfast when Evan calls.

"My car won't start," he says. "Would you be able to pick me up at the station?"

I exhale in relief. I'm not sure why, but I was afraid something bigger would be wrong.

"Sure, no problem," I say.

When I arrive at the subway station, Kim and Evan are already there, chatting and laughing. I'm not late; they're both early. I'm pleased to see them getting along but not terribly surprised, since Evan is the friendliest of my brothers.

He opens the passenger's door and gestures for her to take a seat, then climbs into the back. Before I head to the church, I take a moment to admire Kim. She's wearing a light pink dress with a black ribbon around the waist, and I swear she gets more beautiful every time I see her. I don't know how that's possible, but it's true.

The image of her naked and filthy in bed pops into my mind. I push it aside—now isn't the time for such thoughts.

"You know where you're going?" she asks. "Need me to navigate?"

"No, I'm good."

I start driving. It's a hot, sunny day, rather like Mirabel's wedding; no hint of rain, unlike last time.

"According to Isobel," Evan says, "the rehearsal was a bit of a mess."

"In what way?" I ask.

"People kept missing cues, Auntie Gladys and Yvonne's mother almost came to blows...I don't know. I didn't ask for all the details. Then some of the food at dinner was improperly cooked and had to be sent back. Nolan nearly swallowed a bone then threw up, narrowly missing Yvonne."

Well, that certainly doesn't sound pleasant.

"Is he okay now?" I ask.

"Yep, apparently he's excited about his ring bearer duties, though he's confused at the lack of bears."

When the three of us walk up to the church, Nolan runs down the steps, his mothers just behind him, and grabs my leg. "Uncle Max! Can we play hide and seek? Please?"

"Not now, pumpkin," Daisy says. "You can play later."

For a split second, I worry Nolan won't take this well, but he swiftly moves on.

"I almost swallowed a chicken bone yesterday." He speaks proudly. "Has that ever happened to you?"

"I can't say it has."

"Max! Kim!" Auntie Gladys hurries toward us. "I knew it would work out between you two. Good thing I made you sit at the same table last time. I bet you never would have—how do you say it?—made a move if it hadn't been for my interference." She beams at me. "Perhaps next year, we can celebrate your marriage?"

Nolan sticks his hand in the air and jumps up and down. "I'll be your ring bear! Or flower boy! I have lots of practice."

"I'll keep that in mind," I say.

I put my arm around Kim. I suspect she doesn't enjoy this discussion of our marriage. It doesn't bother me, but I can't blame her.

Fortunately, my aunt soon runs off, saying she needs to help the bride, whose mother, apparently, cannot be trusted. Not surprising that they got in a fight last night.

When we step inside the church, we're immediately greeted by Kim's parents.

"Will you two be next?" her mom asks.

"It's too soon to think about that," Kim replies.

"Just because it's soon doesn't mean it can't happen. I have a colleague whose husband proposed six weeks after they met. They're still married twenty-five years later." She looks meaningfully at me.

"I'll take that into consideration," I say. "Nice to see you again."

"You must sit with us." She touches Kim's arm. "No—maybe you should sit with Max's family. Get to know them better."

"Uh, yes," Kim says. "We'll do that. See you later, Mom."

I steer Kim away from her family. I'm a little overwhelmed by all the people—this is a bigger wedding than any of the others I've attended this year—but I'm most concerned about my date. I hope this wedding is more enjoyable for her than the last one, which featured that painful dinner. I don't know what might happen, but something can always go wrong, and our new relationship feels fragile; I don't know what it can withstand.

As we start walking down the aisle, my father waves to us. Just as I'm about to tell Kim that we can sit wherever she likes, she heads toward my parents. We take our seats and I get a text from Leo, saying he got a speeding ticket and will be late. He probably won't make it in time for the ceremony at two thirty.

The rest of us are here, though: me, Kim, Mom, Dad, Evan, and Jon, all sitting in the same pew, all wearing nice clothes for the last wedding of the summer.

I'll be rather glad to have the weddings over and done with, truth be told.

"Hey, Max." Aaron taps me on the shoulder as he slides into the pew behind me—he and Rory are on time today, just barely. Rory is still knotting his tie. "How are you?"

Before I can answer, the organ music begins.

Chapter 30

Kim

THE FIRST BRIDESMAID WALKS regally down the aisle. She's wearing a blue dress and carrying a bouquet of white and pale purple flowers. The bridesmaid's dress is lovely, even nicer than what Tessa had us wear. The flowers—the bouquets, as well as the ones decorating the ends of the pews and the altar—are similarly exquisite.

The next bridesmaid enters and walks toward the front, followed by the third. They all have updos with a few lose curls to frame their faces. They're followed by another woman in a blue dress, who I presume is the maid of honor, based on the number of men—four—standing beside the groom at the front of the church. She, too, is smiling, but there's something about it that looks strained.

I attribute it to a long day. The rehearsal dinner was last night, and they were probably up early this morning to start makeup and such.

Behind the maid of honor is Nolan, carrying a pillow with the wedding bands. I wouldn't trust a three-year-old with expensive jewelry, but he walks happily down the aisle without any shenanigans. Daisy, in the row in front of us, lets out an audible sigh of relief when he makes it to the front.

Next are three little girls in white dresses, somewhere between the ages of three and six, each holding a small bouquet. Everyone coos over how sweet they are. At one point, the middle girl slows down and the last girl bumps into her, but that tiny imperfection just makes it better. Makes it *real*.

Then the music changes and the bride enters—

No, where is the bride?

She seems to be a few beats behind, but there she is now, walking down the aisle in a stunning white dress and veil. Her skin is flawless and glowing.

I turn toward the altar, to Carl, who's watching his wife-to-be. I saw Carl a couple of times a year as a kid, but I don't know him well now. I never particularly liked him, truth be told. He was the kind of boy who made fun of you and played pranks that weren't at all amusing, but I'm sure he's better as an adult.

I don't understand why he isn't completely blown away by Yvonne. Or maybe he is and I'm just too far away from him to tell.

Yvonne's pace seems to slow, and when she passes our pew, I have the distinct feeling that something isn't right. I'm the closest to the aisle—Max insisted I sit here—so I have a good view of her expression. She's smiling, but her lips are trembling, and her hands are shaking on the bouquet. Everything about her looks pulled taut, pulled to its breaking point.

Well, planning a wedding is stressful, and dealing with the demands of family isn't easy. There are so many decisions to be made, so many things to argue about: venue, date, guest list, food, dress... In fact, the more I think about planning a wedding, the more overwhelming it sounds. I mean, my mother and I rarely agree, plus there's the groom and his family.

I glance over at Max. Do I really know what I'm doing here? I can't imagine going through the hassle of a wedding.

And then there's marriage.

Even if your wedding day is stressful, shouldn't you at least be excited about spending your life with your new spouse?

I'm suddenly convinced that Yvonne isn't excited. Beneath the veneer of poise and beauty, I'm positive she's scared shitless on what is supposed to be the happiest day of her life.

That's the fantasy we're sold, isn't it? The happiest day of your life. A whole industry dedicated to providing that for you.

But something is deeply wrong. I didn't feel that way at Isobel's, Mirabel's, or Tessa's wedding, yet I can't stop feeling that way now.

Or am I projecting my own issues onto Yvonne? Maybe she's doing just fine. I've barely talked to her before; I don't know her. I just know myself, and I know I don't want a packed church wedding like this. I don't want to be tied to another family, don't want to be slowly worn down by a long-term relationship. I don't want to lose myself in a marriage.

I was happy by myself, dammit. I went out, I had fun, I had sex.

Okay, there's more sex—amazing sex—now that I'm dating Max, and we have fun together...but will it stay this way?

One-night stands were definitely easier.

Then I think of waking up next to him. Dinner in bed. The way he held me close under his big umbrella as we walked to the restaurant in Little Italy; the way it felt safe.

The way he said "I love you" when he thought I was sleeping.

But when I replay those words in my mind now, my skin chills despite the warm weather. I'm not ready for this.

Seriously, what the hell am I doing? I swore off relationships for a good reason, and then I ignored my own rules.

I'm in too deep now. I let him wreck me with pleasure; I let him destroy my defenses with his serious thoughtfulness.

"Are you okay?" Max murmurs, handing me a tissue.

Shit, there are tears streaking my face.

"Yeah, I'm fine," I say automatically as everyone takes a seat. Why does he have to be so damn kind?

I look forward, and I can't help the words that are running through my head.

Don't marry him. Don't do it. Don't do it.

I'm not sure whether it's for myself or for Yvonne.

"We are gathered here today..." the minister begins.

And then Yvonne bolts.

Chapter 31

Max

As Yvonne hurries up the aisle, a collective gasp goes up through the room. In the front row, Auntie Gladys shrieks and collapses into my uncle's arms.

This is the first time I've been to a wedding with a runaway bride.

"Holy shit," Aaron whispers behind me.

Jon seems amused, chuckling under his breath. Figures. Evan looks concerned. Leo is still dealing with his speeding ticket, I guess. He has yet to make an appearance.

And me? I'm thinking about Kim doing this.

We haven't been together for long; it's too soon to think about getting married, no matter what her mother says. But that's what I want, one day, and I love her.

I want it to be her, this woman who doesn't view me simply as an appropriate guy her parents would approve of. This bold, beautiful woman who's clear about her wants and needs, who crackles with energy and life.

And, unfortunately, I can imagine her bolting.

I would be devastated.

She probably wouldn't do it at the wedding—Kim wouldn't get that far. She told me that she had serious doubts about relationships, yet I still asked her out.

Was I foolish to think it could ever work?

I want to wipe the tears from her face, but I know she won't allow that intimacy right now, and I can't help feeling like those tears have something to do with me.

I don't know how to reassure her, but I want to. I want her to know that I will do everything I can to make her happy—as long as she doesn't want there to be more distance between me and my family. I know she's had issues with partners' families in the past, but as long as mine is good to her, she wouldn't make me do that, would she?

I don't think so, but...

It's silly to be more concerned about Kim leaving me than what's happening in front of my eyes. My cousin has been left at the altar. His groomsmen slap him on the back and murmur words of...I don't know what.

Yvonne's bridesmaids are still at the front of the church, talking amongst themselves. None of them make a move to follow her, which strikes me as odd. Surely one of them would want to go to her now?

Finally, one bridesmaid speed-walks out of the room, but everyone else remains put, including Yvonne's parents. Some people's faces are still frozen in shock, and others start whispering, a mix of English and Cantonese slowly growing in volume.

"How could she do this to him?" someone asks.

My hands clench in my lap. I'm uncomfortable with how they're speaking about Yvonne when they probably don't know the whole situation. Carl has always been my least favorite cousin, and it isn't hard to believe that he wasn't a great fiancé.

"Aiyah," my mother says, and then, to my surprise, she gets up and heads to the door.

Kim scrambles to her feet.

"Where are you going?" I whisper, reaching for her hand.

She shakes her head and follows my mother.

Chapter 32

Kim

I'm not entirely sure why I'm following Lynne, but I am.

"Poor girl," Lynne mutters when I catch up to her.

"Do you know her well?" I ask. "Do you know why she ran?"

Lynne says nothing as heads to the staircase that leads to the basement. Though I suspect Yvonne has already left the building, I go with Lynne. She checks the rooms on the left side of the hallway; I check the rooms on the right.

Yvonne's not in the women's washroom. She's not in the men's washroom. The next door is locked, but I think I hear a noise from the end of the hall. I push open the door to a room that looks like a Sunday school classroom, children's art decorating the walls.

And there she is.

The bride is sitting down. I think she's on a small chair meant for a child, but I can't see the chair with the poof of her dress. I gesture to Lynne, and we enter the room together.

"I'm not going back," Yvonne says when she lifts her head.

Lynne pulls out another small chair and sits next to Yvonne. "Are you sure you don't want to get married?"

"Yes." Yvonne's response is instant. Confident.

I can't imagine getting this close to marriage and not doing it.

"Are you here to change my mind?" Yvonne asks. "For your nephew's sake? To save face?"

Lynne snorts. "What happened? If you want to tell us." She looks at me, then turns back to Yvonne.

Yvonne doesn't immediately reply, and my pulse quickens as I wait for an answer, as I wait to understand what happened. I'm not sure we'll get all the details, but I sense she wants to talk. I take a seat.

"I couldn't sleep at all last night," she says, "and as I was walking down that aisle, I felt like I was marching toward my doom. I know that sounds dramatic, but it felt like...my life was over. I don't want any of this." She gestures to her bouquet on the table beside her, then her big skirts. "I only went along with it because it's what I was supposed to do. I've always done what I'm supposed to, but I just...can't. Not anymore. Gladys is probably in hysterics upstairs. My mom must be wondering how I could do such a thing. The truth is...I don't give a shit."

Lynne chuckles and pats Yvonne's hand.

"Let them talk. I don't care." Yvonne speaks self-assuredly, but then she bursts into tears. "How did I let it get to this point?"

My heart squeezes. It seems like she's spent her life being the perfect daughter, the one who made her parents proud. I have no idea what she does for work, but I suspect she has a good job.

"What about Carl?" Lynne asks gently.

"Fuck Carl." Yvonne swipes at the tears streaming down her face.

I reach into my purse and hand her a tissue.

She nods in thanks. "He barely did anything for the wedding, and he acted like he was doing me a favor by letting me figure out every detail. I was constantly arguing with both of our mothers, who didn't approve of any of my decisions, while he did nothing to support me."

Yeah, that doesn't sound fun.

"I know that's what marriage would be like, too," she says. "I would do everything. He wants to start trying for a baby right away, and I bet I'd do all the childcare. It would all be on *me*. Like it was on my mother, and now she acts like I owe her. I'm not sure what I want, but I don't want that. I don't think I want to get married to anyone."

My instinct is to protest, even though I've said similar things in the past, but I keep my mouth shut.

"He's not even that great in bed," Yvonne continues. "I've only slept with three men, and none of them have been great."

Again, definitely not like Max. The first time was nothing special, but it's good now—and I've slept with many men, so I have lots to compare to.

"Or maybe that's just the way sex is for me?" She frowns, then looks horrified, as if she just realized what she said out loud. "Auntie, I'm sorry...I shouldn't...especially in a church..."

"Ah, don't worry about it," Lynne says. "It's fine. I'm not telling anyone."

Yvonne glances at the floor. "While I was having my hair done this morning, I looked up divorce articles and statistics. Lots of women are happier after divorce. They feel relieved. Is that what marriage is always like?"

"I've been married for almost forty years, and I wouldn't be happier without my husband."

"But what if I'm waiting for the impossible? What if my standards are too high? What if I want someone perfect, someone who doesn't exist?"

Lynne arches a brow. "Is that the problem? Carl isn't perfect? I think it's more than that."

"I feel like he doesn't even know me," Yvonne whispers.

"You should wait for the right person," Lynne says. "But first, you should get out of here. Do you have your phone and wallet?"

Yvonne nods and holds up a small purse.

"Take my car." Lynne fishes her keys out of her pocket.

My eyes widen, as do Yvonne's.

"Auntie," she says, "I can't—"

"Obviously, you will return it. Sometime in the next few days, when you're ready. It's the Camry in the back right corner of the lot." Lynne finds some crayons and paper in the room, writes down a number, and stuffs it in Yvonne's purse. "Now go. I'll pretend I didn't see you. Well, I have to tell my husband because he'll wonder about the car, but I won't tell your mother or Carl's mother."

"But she's your sister-in-law."

"We never got along," Lynne says dismissively. "Just text your mom so she knows you're alive. She'll worry. But you should go now, if you don't want to be found." She points to the right. "There's a small door at the far end of the hallway. Try that rather than going up the main staircase."

Yvonne gives Lynne a quick hug before dashing out of the room.

Now I'm alone with Max's mom, and my mouth is hanging open.

"What is it?" she asks.

"You just encouraged her to leave her own wedding."

"She clearly didn't want to get married. I should have told her to go back down the aisle?"

I'm struck by how different Lynne is from my own mother. If my mom were confronted with a runaway bride, she'd tell the poor woman to think about what this would do to her family, think about what people would say.

She wouldn't give the bride her fucking car keys.

The wild thing is, within the same conversation, Lynne implied she's happily married.

"Lynne, can I ask you something?"

"Go ahead," she says.

"You really don't regret getting married?"

"No."

"What about dealing with your husband's family? You don't get along with his brother's wife. How about his parents?"

"My mother-in-law didn't like me until I gave birth to her first grandson, followed by three more boys. Gladys has never forgiven me for that." She shrugs. "I manage. I don't regret marrying him instead of the man I was supposed to..."

"Wait, who were you supposed to marry?"

There's a split second of panic on her face. "Forget I said that."

I'm not sure I'll be able to, but I nod. Does Max know about this?

"So. Uh." I have more I want to say, but it takes a moment to find my words. "Was your husband mad that you didn't get along with your mother-in-law? Did he tell her about all your problems?"

"Ah, once he got mad at me for something, but only once. I was pretty rude, so, I can't blame him. He always had my back. That's the most important thing."

And that was the problem with Troy. It didn't feel like he had my back—with his family, or in general. With his mother, it felt like I was being thrown to the wolves.

Max is close to his family, yes, but he wouldn't stand for them mistreating me. Even if he feels extra responsibility as the oldest son, I can't imagine him forcing me to grit my teeth and bear it over and over.

And really, Lynne seems quite lovely. I think we could get along. She might not make a warm and friendly first impression, but she's been kind and understanding today—I can see the similarities between her and Max. She listened to Yvonne, rather than pressing ahead with her own agenda, and she listened to me, too.

My mother doesn't pay attention to me like that; it feels as if she's never really seen me, never cared about my own wishes. I've given up on expecting anything else from her.

I used to dread having to deal with someone else's family on a regular basis, and I particularly dreaded having a mother-in-law similar to my own mom. Like Troy's mother, unfortunately—they have a lot in common. Troy's mom didn't see me as my own person. I suspect Mom wouldn't treat a daughter-in-law well, either; she'd likely be better with a son-in-law.

Yes, I've had bad luck with the families of the men I've dated, and that's across a variety of cultural backgrounds, but I know not all parents are the same. I mean, I've had things go wrong with a partner's family in a bunch of different ways.

Tessa and Iris, who also have Asian mothers, didn't have experiences like mine. Tessa is close to her mom. Iris's relationship with her mother has had its ups and downs, and sure, her mother can be overbearing at times, but they've had real heart-to-heart talks, the sort I couldn't dream of having with my mom.

"Is something wrong, Kim?" Lynne's eyebrows draw together. "Why are you asking me these questions?"

"Just some problems I've had with men in the past," I say vaguely, hoping that's enough. "But Max has been wonderful to me, I promise."

"I think he'd make a good partner, and I'm not just saying that because he's my son."

"It doesn't seem like you've ever insisted he get married or have kids."

"I don't want to pressure him. What if he ends up with the wrong person?" She pauses. "I know Max worries about me. He's sensitive. Ever since my youngest was born..." She shakes her head. "He grew up too early. At the time, I was thankful, but later, I saw it was too much. He almost never says no when we ask for something, and it would be easy to take advantage of that, but I try not to."

I nod. I can believe that now.

"In some families," she says, "the mother-in-law is a bully, and the daughter-in-law is expected to take on endless chores and be respectful no matter what, but I want you to know...I would never wish it to be that way."

I blow out a breath. "I appreciate that. Thank you."

Will there still be some negotiation of boundaries? Probably. But I want to be a part of this family, I want to figure out how to make it work with Max and everyone who's important to him.

I don't want to run.

There's a benefit, of course, to close extended families, but if you have a toxic family, it can be a noose. It might seem silly to think about this when we haven't been dating very long, yet I can't help it, due to past experiences. And as my own mother keeps reminding me, I'm getting old.

Even if Max's family wasn't great, though, it might still work between us because he wouldn't let them wear me down. The relationship wouldn't come at a net cost to me. He'd stand up for me—I'm sure of that now.

But I'm glad Lynne and I see eye to eye. It makes things easier. I haven't spent as much time with Howie, but so far, I'm hopeful.

"I don't want to interfere in your relationship," Lynne says, "but I'd like to get to know you better, yes? And not at some painful dinner that Gladys has arranged."

I fail to hold back an inelegant snort.

Just as I'm about to speak, there's some commotion in the hallway. To be honest, I'm surprised it took so long.

"Lynne!" Gladys barks from the door to the room. "What are you doing here?"

"Kim and I are just chatting," Lynne replies.

"Have you seen Yvonne? Was she here?"

"No. I have no idea where she went."

Gladys hurries off.

"You know," Lynne says to me, "I wouldn't have tried to find Yvonne if her bridesmaids had followed her. I hardly know her. But they're her bridesmaids! Whose side are they on?" She struggles to get up from the very low chair, and I jump to my feet and help her. "Thank you. I hope it works out between you and my son—"

"We haven't been together for long."

"I know, but I can see the way he looks at you. I wouldn't be surprised if he asks you to marry him one day."

I can't help the curl of warmth inside me. It honestly *delights* me that he might propose someday, and isn't that a strange feeling for someone who was against long-term relationships not long ago?

We exit the room together. Upstairs, it's pandemonium, and Lynne and I get separated. I search for Max, suddenly desperate to find him, to feel his arms around me.

When I don't see him, I head outside. Less than an hour has passed since we got here, but it feels like it's been much, much longer.

And there he is, standing in the garden.

Chapter 33

Max

Kim runs toward me. When she left, it felt like she was leaving me, like Yvonne hurrying away from Carl. I knew I was probably worrying needlessly, but I couldn't help it. Even if she didn't leave me today, I kept thinking about her doing it in the future.

But now, she throws her arms around me.

"Where did you go?" I ask.

"We found Yvonne downstairs, and your mother told her not to get married if she didn't want to, then handed over her car keys."

I can't help chuckling.

"The two of us talked a bit afterward, and I decided..."

My heart hammers as I wait for her to finish. I brush a lock of hair away from her face; my hand is shaking.

"I'm all in," she says. "When we met, I wasn't interested in anything serious, but that's changed. You've opened my eyes to what a relationship can be."

My face splits into a grin. "What happened in the church basement?"

It's her turn to chuckle. "I realized just how different it is with you. Before, I hoped it could be different, but I struggled to believe that was truly possible. Now, I'm confident in us. Navigating a life with you won't make me feel like I'm compromising myself—"

"I'd never want you to do that," I murmur, holding her close.

"I know. I trust you, Max. And I'm on your side, no matter what."

She stands on her toes, and just as our lips are about to meet, I hear a most unwelcome voice.

"Kim!"

I turn to see her parents.

"I've been looking everywhere for you," Kim's mother says. "How could she do this to him? Do you think they'll still have the banquet? The food is already paid for, yes?"

"I don't know, Mom," Kim replies, "but I'm not going. Max and I have plans."

"How do you have plans? This wedding was your plan for the day."

"I'll talk to you tomorrow, okay?"

Kim returns her attention to me and shoots me a wicked smile. She brushes her lips over mine and—

"Max!"

Oh, God. Now it's my parents. Why can't I just kiss my girlfriend in peace?

"Yes, Dad?" I try not to sound too annoyed.

"I'm sorry to interrupt"—he doesn't sound all that sorry, just amused—"but apparently our car is gone and we'll need a ride home."

"I'll be right there," I say, then press a quick kiss to Kim's lips. "After we drive everyone back, we'll spend some time together, okay?"

She nods. "Sounds good to me."

Evan hurries down the steps of the church. "You didn't forget about me, did you? I'd go with Jon, but he's chatting someone up."

Of course he is. I wonder if my youngest brother will ever change.

The three of us walk across the parking lot, my parents a few steps ahead of us. I keep my arm around Kim because I don't want to let go of her.

My mom suddenly stops, and the rest of us follow suit. "I don't understand. Our car is still here." She gestures to their beige Camry.

"Maybe Yvonne couldn't find it?" I say. "Did you tell her which one?"

"I said it was the Camry in the back corner. If she was in the right area, she would have hit the button to unlock the doors and found it, yes? But I don't see her anywhere."

We all look around the parking lot. Indeed, there's no bride to be found.

"I hope she's okay," Mom says.

"What about Leo?" Evan asks. "He never showed up after the speeding ticket, did he?"

Huh. I hope nothing bad happened. "I'll text him."

"I guess we don't need a ride after all." Dad pulls his keys out of his pocket. "Evan, we'll take you, too. Let them be alone." He tilts his head in my direction and winks.

My face heats, but I certainly don't object to this plan.

"Next weekend," Mom says, "would you two like to come over for a meal? Whichever day works best for you." She looks at Kim, then me.

"Sounds good," Kim says. "How about Sunday?"

They give each other a quick smile, and I can't help smiling, too.

·❤·❤·❤·❤·❤·

As soon as Kim and I are inside my apartment, we take off our shoes and she jumps on me. I grab her ass and press her against the door as we kiss, unable to get enough of each other.

She's here. With me. And she intends to stay.

I think now might be the time to say—

"I love you," she says before I can speak.

Hearing those words from her lips...I can't begin to describe what it means. I feel like I'm filled with light.

"I love you, too." I bury my face in her hair.

"I know. I heard you say it last weekend."

"I thought you were asleep."

"No," she says. "Just like I wasn't asleep when you left the room after Tessa and Malcolm's wedding."

"I hope those words didn't scare you."

"Maybe a little, but it's okay. We're fine now. Much better than that, in fact." She rolls her hips against mine, and I'm instantly rock hard. "And I'll be even better once you're inside me."

I set her down and open my pants.

Her eyes widen. "Right here?"

"Unless you don't—"

"No, no, I do."

I shove the crotch of her panties aside, then pick her up. With no preparation, I impale her on my cock. She screams, and I cover her mouth with one hand, keeping the other hand firmly under her ass.

"We're right next to the hallway," I murmur. "That's it. You can take it."

With her, I feel like I can let go, in a way I've never been able to do with anyone else.

I fuck her roughly as I slip my finger into her mouth. Once she swirls her tongue around it, I move it between her legs and touch her clit.

"I'm not going to last long," I say, "but I'll take care of you, I promise."

She feels so good and tight and wet. It really won't take long at all. She claws at my shoulders, and her mouth is open in pleasure, but she's restraining herself from making any noise.

She's so fucking hot.

Her inner muscles squeeze me, and she allows a soft sound of ecstasy to fall from her lips.

That's all it takes. I empty myself inside her.

And then I take her to the bedroom, set my mouth on her, and make her come.

Afterward, we have a leisurely hour in bed, just holding each other and lazily kissing. I never want this to end, but unfortunately, food will soon become a necessity.

"What do you want for dinner?" I ask.

Kim sits up, and I momentarily forget about my question as I admire the swell of her breasts. She sees me looking and laughs.

"I'll take care of dinner," she says. "You stay here and relax."

"Don't clean any of my pots and pans. Some of them need to be treated carefully."

"I'm not cooking tonight, don't worry. But you can explain it to me later." She presses a finger to my mouth.

After putting on the dress she wore earlier, she leaves. I feel a little weird about the situation. I'm used to preparing food and getting things done, especially in my own apartment.

Without Kim here, staying in bed has lost most of its appeal, so I get dressed—shorts and a T-shirt, not my suit—and clean up the mess we made in our rush to tear off each other's clothes. Once everything has been set to rights, I read a little before putting on the kettle for tea.

She returns just before the water boils, carrying a bag with cold noodles and other dishes from one of the nearby Korean restaurants. She also has a box from a bakery.

Once she's set the food down, I kiss her. It hasn't been long since I last saw her, but I want to touch her as much as possible. I can't get enough of this woman.

She giggles as she opens up the box. "It's a rhubarb vanilla custard tart. Since you like strawberry rhubarb pie, I thought—"

"I love you, did I tell you that?"

She keeps laughing as I kiss her neck.

Everything seems perfect and effortless right now. It won't always be that way, but I know it will always be worth it, as long as I'm with her. I trust we'll be able to talk and figure everything out. I trust we'll take care of each other.

She takes the tart out of the box. "How about we eat dessert first?"

What an appalling, chaotic suggestion. I'm sure she's saying that just to piss me off, but I give her what she wants.

A stern glare.

Epilogue

Kim

THE SATURDAY OF THE Thanksgiving weekend is a beautiful, sunny October day. North of Toronto, the maple trees are orange and red, and it's just warm enough to have lunch on the patio at the hotel where I first met Max. He says the first words he heard out of my mouth were "fucking hell," which sounds about right.

Unlike that day in June, we're not dressed up for a wedding; I'm wearing jeans and a light sweater, and Max is similarly casual. We peruse the menu as we wait for our friends.

It's been several weeks since the fourth wedding of the year, the wedding that didn't actually happen. Despite my lack of recent experience with relationships, everything is going well. I've had dinner with his family a couple of times, and we're seeing them again tomorrow for our Thanksgiving meal. I'm looking forward to it. I'm also looking forward to visiting my brother out in B.C. next week.

My parents continue to be pleased by my relationship with Max, and Mom fawns all over him. But if she's ever a jerk to my boyfriend, I will shut that down as fast as I can.

I close my eyes and enjoy the warmth of the sun on my hair, the light breeze on my skin. There won't be much more nice weather this year.

Max slides his hand into mine. "You know what you want yet?"

"Nope," I say. "You?"

"Yes. I looked at the menu yesterday."

Of course he did. I open my eyes and smile at him, just as Malcolm and Tessa sit down next to us. We have a prime spot beside the heater. It isn't necessary now, but it might be if the sun decides to hide behind the clouds.

"So, you two really are together," Malcolm says.

"You've known for a while," Max points out.

"I needed to see it to believe it. I couldn't quite imagine it at first, but I get it now." Malcolm slaps Max on the back.

"Well, *I* could imagine it." Tessa smiles at me. "I'm so happy for you."

I'm very happy it worked out, too. Once upon a time, I didn't believe a relationship could be like this for me, but now, I know better.

Under the table, I squeeze my boyfriend's hand.

"How's your brother doing?" Malcom asks Max. "Leo, I mean. After, you know…"

"I'm not sure," Max says. "We'll see tomorrow."

After we have lunch with our friends, we walk around the little lake, then go inside—our room should be ready by now.

"Two room keys?" the man at the front desk says.

I nod. "Yes, please."

When I see which room we're in, I laugh.

We take the elevator up and enter the same room that I stayed in last time. I can't wait to make new memories here, but first…

"I have something for you." I reach into my purse and pull out a small package. This is the first wrapped gift I've given Max. Not that I haven't done and bought things for him before, but this is the first one that's involved wrapping paper and ribbon.

Though it might seem a little generic, I think he'll like it, and I did spend half an hour debating which one to get.

He carefully removes the paper, then opens the box to reveal a tie. His lips twitch. As he holds it up, I know exactly what kind of thoughts are running through his mind.

"But why did you give this to *me*," he says, "when you're the one who will be wearing it tonight?"

"I have no idea what you're talking about."

Ha.

"Kimberly," he says warningly.

"Around my wrists, or to cover my eyes—which would you prefer?"

We do, indeed, have a very, *very* good night together.

And unlike the first time we stayed at this hotel, we wake up in each other's arms.

About the Author

Jackie Lau decided she wanted to be a writer when she was in grade two, sometime between writing "The Heart That Got Lost" and "The Land of Shapes." She later studied engineering and worked as a geophysicist before turning to writing romance novels. Jackie lives in Toronto with her husband, and despite living in Canada her whole life, she hates winter. When she's not writing, she enjoys gelato, gourmet donuts, cooking, hiking, and reading on the balcony when it's raining.

To learn more and sign up for her newsletter,
visit jackielaubooks.com.

Also by Jackie Lau

Donut Fall in Love Series
Donut Fall in Love
The Stand-Up Groomsman

Weddings with the Moks Series
Four Weddings to Fall in Love

Chu's Restaurant Series
The Sitcom Star
The Reluctant Heartthrob

Cider Bar Sisters Series
Her Big City Neighbor
His Grumpy Childhood Friend
Her Pretend Christmas Date (novella)
The Professor Next Door
Her Favorite Rebound
Her Unexpected Roommate

Kwan Sisters/Fong Brothers Series
Grumpy Fake Boyfriend
Mr. Hotshot CEO
Pregnant by the Playboy
Bidding for the Bachelor

Holidays with the Wongs Series
A Match Made for Thanksgiving
A Second Chance Road Trip for Christmas
A Fake Girlfriend for Chinese New Year
A Big Surprise for Valentine's Day

Baldwin Village Series
One Bed for Christmas (prequel novella)
The Ultimate Pi Day Party
Ice Cream Lover
Man vs. Durian

Chin-Williams Series
Not Another Family Wedding
He's Not My Boyfriend

Kobo Originals
The Unmatchmakers
Not Your Valentine

* 9 7 8 1 9 8 9 6 1 0 3 1 2 *